Offbeat

Jen Lowry

Monarch Educational Services, L.L.C.
Clayton, NC

Offbeat
by Jen Lowry

Cover Designer: Jen Lowry - Monarch Educational Services, L.L.C.

https://jenlowrywrites.com/   @jenlowrywrites
Offbeat/Jen Lowry. – First Edition 2020
Library of Congress Control Number:2019921274
Summary: Mary Oxendine is on top of the charts and should be on top of the world. For the past five years, she's gained millions of fans, adoring her every move as she rocks the stage as Mary Bella. They don't know she's hurting. No one knows just how much she's losing parts of herself. She's angry. She's bitter. Will she compromise it all for fame or will she have the courage to face the true music within?

ISBN for paperback version: ISBN: 978-1-7331381-8-5
{1. Christian Fiction 2. Clean Fiction 3. Romance 4. Clean Romance 5. Christianity 6. Faith 7. Musician 8. Suspense 9. Relationships 10. Holiday 11. Family Drama 12. Pop Star 13. Diverse

Typography by Monarch Educational Services, L.L.C.

7 6 5 4 3 2 1

Monarch Educational Services, L.L.C.
Clayton NC

Offbeat

Jen Lowry

Monarch Educational Services, L.L.C.
Clayton NC

Books by Jen Lowry
The Sunday Killer (Releasing August 31, 2021)
The Hartwell Chronicles Teenage Exorcist Series
My Boyfriend's Back Angels in Love Series
Lyric Harper & the Harmonic Bridge
The Raptor Revolution: Save Christmas Mountain
Bridges, Crossings, & Tides - The Lightbearers Series
A Magical Christmas Wedding
Sweet Potato Jones
The Monarch Method: How to Write a Novel From
Start to Finish

Dr. Jennifer Ikner Lowry
Challenge Devotional Series
Happy Renewal Year
Everyday Mom Challenge
30 Day Teacher Challenge
Fingerprint Curriculum
Everyday Author Challenge Bible Devotional

The Clay in the Potter's Hand: Southern Poetry
Fact vs. Fiction: Southern Poetry

To Eli, for dreaming with me
To Solomon and Samuel, my loves forever
To Aunt Dot, for always believing in me

How Do I Love Thee? (Sonnet 43)
Elizabeth Barrett Browning - 1806-1861

How do I love thee? Let me count the ways.
I love thee to the depth and breadth and height
My soul can reach, when feeling out of sight
For the ends of being and ideal grace.
I love thee to the level of every day's
Most quiet need, by sun and candle-light.
I love thee freely, as men strive for right.
I love thee purely, as they turn from praise.
I love thee with the passion put to use
In my old griefs, and with my childhood's faith.
I love thee with a love I seemed to lose
With my lost saints. I love thee with the breath,
Smiles, tears, of all my life; and, if God choose,
I shall but love thee better after death.

Missing Pieces Come Back

There was a wanting Mary experienced every time she heard the final chords of the guitar solo of her last song on the set. She felt she needed more, but with a twenty-thousand-sold-out arena of screaming fans adoring her, the thoughts made her feel guilty, and she tried her best to push them aside.

Did she need more music? Could she extend the show even longer? She couldn't figure out what the more was, but it nagged against her heart, pulling at it like a little frayed-edge string always wanting to be toyed with.

"Great show, babe. Best one on the tour so far."

Mary smirked. "You always say that, Riff. Seriously, after every show, for the past five years."

"Well, I can't lie, can I? Straight facts, Princess Mary Bella."

She wanted to say, I'm sure you can, and do it well, but refrained. She wasn't in the mood for one of her manager's dramatic tantrums, and he could have them, like nobody's business.

A family was waiting for her in the wings, and she squeezed Mark's arm, her burly Scottish assistant, who'd been taking care of them for the show.

Mary whispered, "Thanks for babysitting."

"It's been a joy like no other."

She approached the young fan, clasping tight to a handmade sign with purple and black paint that read Mary Makes the World Go Round, the title of her newest album, and prayed for strength to at least smile. There was a sense of overwhelming loss when she looked at the child, and she didn't even know her or the family. The weight of it all felt like an anchor around her neck, and she felt for it, only to hit her charm necklace peeking through her tiger clawed ripped t-shirt.

It had taken two months with her agent going back and forth with the Make-A-Dream Organization to make all of the arrangements for their day, and Mary Bella had actually forgotten she'd agreed to it. The family was set up with a dinner before the show in one of the backstage dressing rooms, but Mary rarely ate before a concert—, taking shots and IV infusion drips were more the new craze of stardom schedules.

Maybe that's what she was missing, not being able to give back more. The more money she earned, the more tours they added, the less light of day she saw, with the chaos ever rolling around her like a constant thunderstorm.

Her eyes focused on the sweet innocence of the child, and all of her wanting more left her the minute the fan's delicate voice said, "That was a dream come true, Mary Bella."

"Just call me Mary, remember. That's my stage name. You don't have to tell the world, though. They don't know all of my secrets. Do you want a secret stage name?"

"How about plain Josey Wales? My Daddy named me after his favorite old western. I'm no outlaw, and ain't rough and tough at all, but I still love my name."

Mr. Wales laughed. "Well, you were born the day they did the Clint Eastwood marathons, and we already came with the last name, so it was fate, I tell you. It was hands down fate. You can't mess with your date with fate."

"I think Josey Wales is a fine stage name. It sounds mysterious."

"Oh, do you think so? I think it does. It matters."

"What does?"

"Names matter. Your stage name, Mary Bella, that matters."

Mary replied, "Maybe. Maybe it was one of those just because moments when you don't know why things happen, but they do."

"I know those moments. Kind of feels like one now for our family." The mother turned from her child to Mary. "Thanks so much for agreeing to do this. All through the chemo treatments and hospital stays, you've stayed with her, and your music kept pushing her on."

"I know every song by heart," said the child, who looked like her last days may be fast approaching.

Mary said a quick prayer for healing, and then she felt an idea growing. Maybe she could pull it off. She looked through the curtain and saw most of her audience was still sticking around, taking selfies, and recording reviews of the show to post online.

"Do you happen to know We Just Met, Watch Out? That's one I didn't sing tonight."

The girl squealed with absolute delight. "Of course, I do! I love that song!"

"I know this wasn't in the plans, but would you like to come out on stage, and sing it with me?"

Josey's eyes lit with an excitement out of control, then slowed to a dull aching pain Mary could almost reach out and touch. "I can't. I can't go out like this?"

She put her hand up to her purple scarf and fiddled with it to pull it down further on her forehead.

"Oh, that? No worries about your looks, honey. I think you look divine. I thought you meant you couldn't sing." She winked.

Her mother said, "Oh, no, on the contrary. Our Josey can sing like a little bird on Christmas morning calling her fledglings back for presents."

Josey crinkled up her nose, "A crow."

Her Dad chimed in, "A cardinal."

Mary knew it must have been an inside thing between them because all at once Josey softened. "Okay. Let's do it."

"For real?" asked Mary, surprised her idea actually was heard.

"For real. Hurry, too, before I change my mind."

Mr. Wales already had his recorder out. "I'm capturing this show, for sure as it's rained all day."

"As sure as the moon is out tonight, this one is for the books," whispered the mom, as she hugged Mary too tight for a little too long.

"Okay, let's go before my band packs everything away. This is a first, so give me a second."

Mary sauntered back to her bandmates and gave them a quick talking to. It didn't take any convincing once they turned and saw Josey smiling like she'd won the grand lotto from her wheelchair backstage view. They all had kids and wives back home, even her sax player had a couple of grandkids.

When the crowd realized Mary was back on the stage, the place erupted like a volcano, the pressure having nowhere to go but up and straight to her. She took a couple of steps back to readjust herself to the lights and grabbed the mic.

"Tonight, we've got a special show for all my loyal fans who stuck around a little longer. I've got a singer who I can't wait for you to meet. She's a star in my heart, and I know she'll be your new favorite. Meet Josey Wales, singing with me, We Just Met, You Better Watch Out!"

The crowd went wild when Josey wheeled across the stage. She waved at the girls in the front row, and Mary had a feeling that she knew what she was going to ask when Josey turned to her with those sparkling eyes, magnified by lights and adrenaline.

"Can they come up? Just those girls? The ones right there wearing scarves even though they don't have to. Those are my best friends. They've stuck by me through it all."

"Of course," answered Mary.

She motioned for the paid security to let them through the metal gates, and her bodyguards lifted the young girls onto the stage with ease. They clapped and danced with pure joy when their feet hit the platform.

Mary watched, a little awestruck herself, thinking she was more the fan than they were. When had she felt that kind of freedom?

Maybe that's what she was missing.

The band cranked up the music, and Mary placed the headset mic on Josey and stood close to her, drawing strength from the small child when it should've been the other way around. Mary felt vulnerable and completely alone in that very second between a note and the first line.

She let it hang a second and then was carried away with the lyrics of a song that meant so much to her, but she didn't know why.

There's no time like the present
Why don't we meet
There's no place I'd rather be
Then by your side,
No other place to run
I'll be your girl
Let's have some fun
Because this town is the same ol' same ol'
I'll make your world go round
For now, until forever shatters to brilliance
Until it all melts away
And all that's left is you at the rising sun
Here you come now
I see you walking this way
We just met, you better watch out!

The fans went wild when the mic was left in the hands of Josey Wales, the new outlaw in town with a band of smiling best friends, and parents who couldn't stop crying, cheering, and laughing, emotions mixed all together in a concoction of pride and peace.

Mary waved goodbye to her fans as the lights changed in dramatic fashion, sending her and everyone around her the signal that it was time to move on. Next show. But not like this one. There wouldn't be one like this one.

She stood a minute trying to take it all in and squared her shoulders. It had been a while since she stopped moving to even catch glimpses of the end of things. With the way she was always corralled about, she felt like a bull in a china shop most days: just bumping into things, causing messes that other people were cleaning up before the word got out—all paid for, said and done. Next shop. Next stop.

Josey said, "Thanks for giving me the courage to sing. I've always dreamed about singing on stage, being a star just like you."

"Don't ever dream of being like me. I'm nothing special, just a woman in a leather jacket and some overpriced face cream. Dream of being like you. And how old are you again?"

"I'm twelve," she said. Her voice lowered. "About to be…"

Josey's mom added, "Her birthday is in two months. She's been counting down the days to reaching the teenage mark."

Josey said, "But we don't know if that's coming for me."

"This happened. Who knows what the Lord has in store for you?"

Mary cupped her hand over her mouth. She didn't mean to say the "L" word. She knew how much that could get her in trouble. She'd had the no politics, no religion talks with her manager and agent multiple times, especially when life around her seemed heated in debates about both subjects.

Mrs. Wales said, "I didn't know you were a believer. Josey, did you hear that? She believes in Jesus."

Mary noticed one of the girls with Josey was recording the scene. She barked, her voice rising without control. "Can you please cut that off? Can I not have a private conversation just once?"

Immediately, the girl put the phone down and slid it in her pocket. "I'm sorry."

"Can you show me you will delete it. That's all I ask. I let you come on stage and this is how I get repaid?"

Her face flooded red, and she stammered, "Here...here...I'll show you."

The girl held the phone out to Mary, and she deleted the last video. "I'm sorry I snapped. Will you forgive me?"

Everyone fell awkwardly quiet.

The little girl mumbled, "It's okay."

"Look, it's hard being this way. I was once twelve, without all of this and dreaming about it. Sometimes the saying be careful what you wish for is true. All of my privacy is taken away. I can't be me in a world that doesn't know me."

Mr. Wales patted her on the shoulder. "Well, we know you. What you did for my daughter tonight will last a lifetime for us."

Mary didn't know what prompted her to ask, but it fell out as easy as the "L" word: "Do you have a piece of paper? Two, actually."

Mrs. Wales pulled out a small butterfly notepad from her purse. "Here, dear."

She scribbled her email address on it, folded it up tight, and handed it to Mrs. Wales. "Can you please keep this between us? I trust you. This is my personal email, the one away from all this," she said as she waved her hand back towards the stage. "Can you let Josey email me a time or two, and you guys keep me posted? Maybe send me a couple of recordings of Josey singing a song she wrote, and I can mix them in my next album."

Josey screamed, "You'd do that? You'd really do that? Girls, did you hear that? I could be on the next album!"

"That might just happen. Who knows if I can pull those kinds of magic strings, but I can promise I'll try. Now, this paper is for you."

"Why?"

"Because I want your autograph."

Josey sat back in her chair and smiled. She placed her hand over her heart and did the dramatic eye roll. "Seriously? Did this just happen in my life? Momma, did you hear that? Mary Bella asked for my autograph!"

"Appears to be so. As sure as the rain is falling, take it because it's making flowers grow," said her mother, in the odd way the family always found ways to make statements almost sound like quotes Mary could add to her Pinterest page.

"Well, I'll say, writing Josey Wales on a piece of paper never felt so good?"

"It's never come out that easy before. Especially on the likes of your homework, that's for sure," her father chimed in.

"Nope," she said as she wrote her final overexaggerated loop of the last letter. "I think I need to practice my cursive a little more."

"Maybe that's a good idea. I have a feeling you just might wake up a little famous tomorrow. Who knows how many videos are out there circulating with you singing tonight? You stole the show."

"The show was over. I was just having the time of my life."

"And you gave me something that's been missing."

"But I didn't give you anything." She turned to her mother. "We should have brought her a gift."

"I don't think she meant an object, dear. The kind that doesn't come wrapped in a store."

Mr. Wales laughed. "Now, you sound like the narrator for The Grinch."

"Well, that is what she meant, dear."

"We all knew that."

"Apparently not Josey."

The scene was broken up by Mary's assistant, Mark. "Time to go, crew. We have a car waiting to take ye to the airport. Yer plane leaves in thirty minutes."

"Listen to how he talks, Momma. It's like the movies."

Mark beamed at the little girl. "Ye watched Braveheart, then? I could bore you a little about Scottish history and all of the battles. I'm quite keen on teaching history to young lads or lassies."

Mr. Wales shook Mark's hand and said, "Maybe that's a conversation we could have one day, sir."

Instead of letting her say a proper goodbye, Mark pulled her by the arm and started to steer her as another group of people came to usher the Wales family from the sidelines so they could start breaking down the set.

It wasn't over. Not like that. Mary broke free and gave each one a hug. "Thanks for everything," she whispered to Josey.

Josey's eyes brimmed with tears. "Thank you. This was more than amazing."

"Keep in touch, rock star Josey Wales."

They all waved goodbye and Riff, her manager, who'd now joined the party, leaned in to whisper, "You took that a little too far. You don't know what sickness they have, and you can't catch even the slightest cold."

"Are you really serious right now? Did you just say that?"

Riff took her by the elbow to lead her a little quicker through the back gates. "Yes, I did. We're paid to look out for you. No hugging. No touching, even. No getting too close to people. No promises."

"You heard that, huh?"

"I heard everything. We'll talk about the "L" word later. I can't believe you, Mary. Always pushing against the wind when you need to just learn to go with the flow."

"You mean, your flow."

"Our flow. All of this is for you."

She muttered, "I'm sure."

When Mary was settled in her private plane, she pulled off her too-tall boots and sighed with relief. She hated the costumes they'd started picking for her and thought everything was getting a little too suggestive and outrageous.

"Go with the flow," was Riff's favorite slogan. She should give him a print shop and brand it for him.

She'd been going with the flow for a little too long now, and she knew tonight, standing on that stage in some city she couldn't name, with a child from Make-A-Dream Organization, exactly what it all was that left a void in her heart the size of the Grand Canyon.

Mary grabbed her fuzzy elf socks out of her backpack. She leaned against the cool glass and could almost feel the rain falling against her face.

Almost.

It'd been awhile since she cried.

Cried-like-a-river kind of tears, and tonight was going to be one of those. She had no doubts about that.

Here I Go Again

So much was out of Mary's control, and it didn't dawn on her until she hit the tarmac.

"Stop one hundred and twenty-one," announced her pilot.

Mary asked, "Where are we?"

Riff answered, half asleep, "Somewhere on the East coast. Maybe North Carolina."

"Maybe?"

"Close enough. East coast, west coast, what's the difference? A stadium seating count is all the concern we have, M. Oh, speaking of concern, I heard you slip some vile language last night, and you need to watch it. That girl was recording you."

"God's name isn't vile, Riff. You need to watch it."

"It's vile for your image and would cause damage. You'd separate yourself from millions of fans at the mention of the name, even in passing. They'd put you on a side, the opposite one they're on, and it wouldn't be about your music anymore. It would be about that. You're a star. More than we would've ever imagined. You were nominated for another award, by the way. I forgot in the middle of panicking over the "L" word, which will turn you to loser if you aren't careful," he scolded her as he held the L sign up to his forehead.

"That's old, Riff. Really old."

"And?"

She stood up to stretch and walked up and down the aisle to release the tension in her legs. "I want to see my break schedule."

"Break?"

"Yes, break. I need a break."

"You need to stop at an ATM. That's all. Do you need to go shopping?"

She'd done so much online shopping this year, the thrill of even the purchase left her. "Let me repeat myself. I need time away."

"To do what?"

"Something other than this."

"Ride the Ferris wheel until I say break. We've got to keep this thing turning round and round."

"What if I don't want to go to the Riff amusement park anymore? What if I say close it down?"

He inched closer. "Is that a threat? Don't throw trash at me this early in the morning. I'm not feeling up to being your servant right now."

"I'm just saying I think it's time we slowed down. You heard the pilot. One hundred and twenty-one stops this year."

"It's not like you have family to go to," he remarked, his face darker than it needed to be.

"That was low, Riff. Even for you."

"Facts, M. Facts and bucks. That's what talks."

"I'm just tired."

"Aren't we all," replied Mark, who grabbed her bag from her seat. "And with Christmas coming up and all, ye'll get a few days of absolutely nothin', and then I'll hear how bored ye are."

"Christmas?"

Mary couldn't believe she'd forgotten the holidays. What in the world was the matter with her? She was slowly losing place markers of reality.

Mark said, "Ye act surprised. Ten more shows, and we're calling it a year, Mary. It's almost over, so stop yer whining, and let's do what we have to do today. Tomorrow will fend for itself."

Mary wondered if they had to do it, today or tomorrow. Everyone around her looked and acted miserable. No one even pretending to smile anymore. Five years ago, it was so different. The comradery between bandmates was on point, and she was treated with respect, even at the age of sixteen. She found the more she walked the line, the easier it was for it to become blurred and she was tiptoeing in mist until her direction was lost.

"I need a new navigation," she whispered, to no one in particular. Maybe God. She felt a song starting to build.

> I need a new navigation
> A new sense of direction
> A GPS that makes sense and
> Can figure out the backroads
> That are off the beaten path
> And get me out of the headlights
> Where no heavy traffic treads and

Tramples my sight
All I need is God Pointing Steps
To make it through this life
To lead me where I'm supposed to be led

Lead me where I'm to be led
Not this way I'm traveling but the next
Lead me where I'm supposed to be led

Mark interrupted her music-making. "What are ye humming? I like the tune of that."

"Oh, nothing. It doesn't matter." If she didn't hurry up and write the lyrics down somewhere, they'd be lost in life's translations and turn to white noise before too long.

He said, "None of it does, anymore, does it?"

Mary stood and faced Mark, and for the first time in a really long time, looked at her father's best friend. His bags were growing deeper, wrinkles forming cobwebs around tired, gray eyes.

"You've got more spider webs than before."

"That's what I've always lovingly called me wrinkles. Thanks for pointing the new designs out. Trying to crack jokes now, are ye?"

"No, I didn't mean it like that. I just noticed, that's all."

"Ye noticed something. That's a start. Start noticing," he whispered, and he stepped out of the plane ahead of her to block her from the entertainment news that was waiting for her.

As sure as the rain was falling all day and night across state lines, they'd be there, she thought, taking the words from Mr. Wales.

She loved music. She loved singing. It was all she could ever imagine herself doing but not like this. Her family was amidst a scandal. Mary practically disowned her mother when she discovered she stole half of her money. Lawyers were always hounding her for settlements, and she had a stack of endorsements she'd been holding at bay the second she turned twenty-one. She hadn't even blown out her candles before Riff was handing her a folder with one of his grand ideas inside.

At what cost was she living this life?

Hundreds of reporters were screaming at her for statements, asking what plans did she have for the holidays, and what was up with her and Darian? She tried to control her face but knew it was slipping away with all of her resolve.

She felt the venom rise when one jerk called, "And why did you do a stunt last night with pulling the girl on stage that couldn't sing? Is it because it's up for Song of the Year and you're trying to sway more votes your way? Pathetic, using that child."

Mary spat out fire. "I've never used a child. What are you talking about, Song of the Year?" She turned to Mark and he nudged her from the crowd that was pressing in on them even tighter, closing around them like a boa constrictor. She felt her anger and voice exploding all at once, spewing at the crowd that seemed to overtake her all at once.

One small opening space left to escape through now with the already closing in press or they'd be trapped for the next half hour.

"And she could sing. The girl sang like an angel."

"I bet you don't even remember her name."

"Her name is Josey Wales. Come closer to me so I can make you forget you ever had a name."

Mark leaned in and spoke through clenched teeth, "Ignore them. Take that look off yer face now. They'll capture it. The flashes haven't stopped."

"So, what if they do! Why do people have to be so cruel. She sounded like an angel."

"I agree with ye, but they just want to get a rise out of ye. Yer temper as of late is capturing headlines."

"If they want to see a temper, I'll show them…"

Riff was now between her and the reporters, his hand raised to silence them all as he made his daily report about the happenings of the star in question. He pushed Mark and her through the small opening, and she felt the breeze of the open air.

Mark got her safely out of the way before she could cause any more damage. "Ye need to go get some help with that. I'll get ye a life coach or something. Getting ye to calm down shouldn't be part of an assistant's job. I thought this was just for the coffee runs."

"Funny. You know you do way more for me than just grab my lattes. Speaking of lattes…"

"Yes, Mary. Coming right up."

"That's the spirit."

"Anything the girl wants, the girl gets."

She asked, "Anything?"

"Well, not unless it's on this," he spoke while juggling his overstuffed calendar in his hands, pulling out an agenda and waving it in her face. "If it's not here, then we'll have to call Dot, who has to contact Sam, and then we'll criss-cross applesauce check with Solomon to be sure we don't double book ye."

"Did you just use criss-cross applesauce in a sentence? I had a flashback to when I was five."

"Spiderwebs might be here, but not here," he said as he moved his hands from his face to his heart.

"What's next?"

"Stadium stop, Mary. Like ye thought it would be something new?"

"Exactly my point. What's next for me, Mark?"

"Only ye know the answer to that," he smiled, as he tucked the lists and notebook back into his satchel he had slung around his shoulder. "Just take me with ye when ye go. I'd follow Mary anywhere."

She said, "You're so weird."

"Facts," he answered.

"Stop. Now you're sounding like Riff."

Riff came between them, storming. "More people need to sound like Riff around here! I'm tired of everyone and everything. This is getting out of hand, Mary. You need to…"

"What?"

"Just shut up," he said.

Mary frowned and turned to Mark. "Did he just tell me to shut up? Are you serious?"

Mark held up his hands and started to walk backwards. "Coffee time."

"Wait."

"I'm not getting into the middle of this one."

"Then, take me with you. I think I need to learn to order my own lattes."

"It's about daggone time. Come on. There's always a coffee shop near an airport. I'll call a car."

"You'll do no such thing, Mark. Bring her back here. Don't walk away from me. I'm not finished with her yet."

"Yes, you are," spoke Mary, her voice clear and calm even though the rage burned within her. "You're done, Riff. No one tells me to shut up. You've abused your power over me long enough. You're fired."

"You can't fire me. I made you."

"You didn't make me. You ruined me. I don't even know who I am anymore because of you." She turned to Mark. "Can you call my agent for me and place it on speaker. I want her to hear how I've been treated. In fact, record the call."

Mark said, "My pleasure. Here."

He already had the number dialed and ready. It surprised Mary to see it was on his speed dial. Her heart hammered with great pleasure as she finished the call to Lydia, her friend and agent, who'd been with her since the beginning. She'd wanted to fire Riff for a long time but hadn't had the courage to do it.

Change is coming, she thought.

Mark clapped, along with her band members who had piled around to see the preshow.

Her guitarists, Eddie and Freddie, the twins who'd been with her since day one said, "Good riddance. We can finally get some peace around here."

They both laughed because they often simultaneously spouted out lines. The rest of the crew started to crack up.

The saxophonist, Benny, leaned over and said, "Thanks for the early Christmas present. That man was toxic."

Another band member called out, "To all of us."

"I didn't realize it'd gotten that bad. I thought it was just me he was attacking," she said.

Maybe Mary had been oblivious to a lot of the goings-on about her and her career. She thought of Josey with unsurmountable troubles to have the courage last night to face her self-doubt and wheel onto the stage. She made one dream come true. It was time she started making her own dreams happen, whatever they might be.

She knew her dreams were never this. If they were, this was misguided. Mary knew she needed to find her way back. She'd been lost for too long.

Mark called out as Riff made his way through the terminal, "Good luck finding another celebrity to boss around, Riff. I think yer days are numbered in this business."

"No more talk of Riff. I really need that coffee."

Mark clapped again, and a lighthearted mood fell over them. Removing poisonous vapors from their atmosphere lifted their spirits like a spell had been broken.

Benny said, "And we all need a break. Ten more shows. That's all! And then we can all go home."

Mary tried to put on a smile, but it didn't reach her eyes. What home? Even though Riff was cruel, he was often right. He just didn't have the filter that was needed when communicating with others. Maybe he was the one needing the life coach.

She knew something was going to have to be arranged. She couldn't just sleep on the plane until the new year when the next lineup hit. "I'll start making plans after tonight's show."

"I can help with that, Mary. Just say the word."

"I told you, you were more than just my latte delivery man."

"I'm glad ye finally noticed. Maybe I'll get me a Christmas bonus. I'm thinking of splurging on a big gift soon."

Mary pulled Benny's hat off his head and borrowed Eddie's shades to try to disguise herself. She looked down at her feet and realized she'd forgotten to take off her fuzzy elf socks, and they went up to her knees. She grabbed Mark's arm, and they made their way through the airport and out into the early morning sun. The rain clouds were off in the distance now, and she could see the shimmering line of the rain still falling.

"Don't let the shock obliterate ye, Miss Vampire of the Night."

"No chance. I'm about to live more in the day, I believe. Rain or shine."

"Sing me that childhood song about the spiders and the rain while we head to the nearest spot."

"That will give me away for sure, Mark. I'm trying to lie low and go incognito."

"Is that what ye call wearing that ridiculous oversized hat and sunglasses, not to mention the socks?"

"I would like to drink my coffee in peace."

"Okay, deal. They'll just think ye're my granddaughter, out for a morning coffee stop before Christmas shopping. With all these spiderwebs accumulating, I could catch me a fly lady. Who knows what the future brings?"

For the first time, Mary felt right with the world, leaving behind the jerk of a manager that had calculated too much verbal abuse against her. She knew she had ten more days of shows left, and after that, she wasn't sure what her own future held.

And that was fine with her. How ironic was it that it took Riff exiting her life for her to actually understand the "go with the flow" mantra?

She wouldn't make a t-shirt out of it just yet, but at least she'd try to live that way for today. Let tomorrow worry about itself.

Merv

Mary finished up the last eight shows without much stress. It was routine at this point, and without Riff hollering at her for every turn she might have made offbeat, she felt more alive on stage than ever. Dress the part. Sing two songs. Fall through the stage. Change again. Fly from the rafters on cables. Change again. Through the same steps she'd taken all year, she felt her light grow stronger—especially when the concert halls were filled with decorations and she had glimpses of twinkle lights during take-offs and landings.

The week of Christmas was soon upon the crew. The band members were all sharing their online shopping order sprees to send back to their wives and husbands for quick wrapping. Mary thought it was a little extreme because the more they shared, the more they added to their own lists to see which band's kid had the grandest Christmas.

Mary's agent was meeting her at eight, and since the show was a two o'clock over and done, she felt the need to ask to go out to dinner with Lydia, instead of sitting on the plane before the next take-off for a quick run-down of things. She had to talk about hiring a new manager and financial team. That was going to be a discussion she didn't want to have around any of the guys.

Lydia agreed to meet up at Chopin's, a steakhouse in the city. Mark had everything arranged and agreed to go with Mary and have a bite to eat while they discussed business. Mark had been the best friend of her late father, and he took his role very seriously with Mary. She honestly didn't know what she would've done if Mark had left her support system after her dad died. Her mother had left soon after, saying that traveling the world with a guy named Mitch was more appealing than the hassle of touring and the darkness it could bring with it.

All she wanted was her money, sandy beaches, and a bum. She got it all but lost a daughter. Mary hoped her mother was miserable.

She hadn't spoken to her mom in three years. It was better to keep it that way. She was sure her mother was still enjoying the cash she'd misappropriated from her in her early stages of her career. It was hard to use the word "misappropriation" to describe what her mom did, even though that was the technical term. It was more like "thief and liar."

Mark said, "Ye're looking far away there, Mary. Everything alright, lass?"

"Yeah, just ready for a hiatus. Maybe a vacation of my own needs to be worked out. Where are you going over the holidays?"

"Back to my family in Massachusetts. I haven't seen them in quite a while, for the case of traveling around with ye. My parents are a little on the older end of it, if I might say. It's time they saw their Markie."

She laughed. "Do they still call you that?"

"Sure do. With the high-pitched tone to go with it. Our Markie."

"I bet you still love it."

"Every sound."

"There's Lydia. I see her through the glass, waiting. See the look on her face? Even with a phone stuck to her ear, it's pleasant. I know I'm walking into the fire but going to have a nice dinner among friends."

"Yer daddy, old Buck, he knew how to take care of his baby girl when he put together yer team. Minus Riff that is, but let's not go there. I think yer momma had more sway on that one."

"Yeah, it's easier to blame her. Let's put Riff on her decision-making plate. Let's thank Daddy in heaven again for you and for Lydia."

"Don't start acting sweet on me all of a sudden, Mary. Where's the edge, girl? The rebellion?"

"Um…about that."

Lydia kissed Mark on the cheek. Mary watched as his eyes did this thing. It was a mischievous look. One that spoke volumes.

"It's nice to see both of you again. Sit down, the two of you."

Mark said, "I was going to let you ladies have a go while I found another table for me."

"We wouldn't hear of it," said Mary. "I insist."

"Nope. Catching me a fly lady, remember the conversation?"

Lydia raised her eyebrows and asked with interest and a little bit of regret, "Do you have a date, Mark?"

There it was. She had a look, too. Mary saw it, and she hid a giggle. Lydia had eyes for Mark. All of this time and no one noticed. What else had she missed? Gray was forming between strands of Lydia's blonde hair, and with her eyes the color of the aquamarine sky, they seemed as if they were lighter since the last time they'd met six months ago.

"I just might at the end of this evening. I'm not getting any younger, as this one keeps reminding me on the daily."

"I do not talk about your spiderwebs on the daily. You exaggerate."

Lydia said, "What spiderwebs? I'm scared of spiders. Do you have pet spiders? Then that means…"

Mark said, "No, dear. It's just my name for me wrinkles, that's all. Anyway, I'm going to see if I can look all lonesome at one of those tiny tables by the window, and ye two talk business. I'll see ye soon. Have fun. And Lydia, let her relax. Take it easy on her tonight. I think she's had a rough couple of days."

Lydia said, "How about a stellar year, Mark. Call it stellar."

"I was never the one hard on her to begin with."

"I know, and I thank you for that."

"We're already starting off this conversation with gratitude. I like it."

Mary said, "No, seriously. You dropped everything to fly here, to where are we again?"

"Raleigh, North Carolina, Mary. You really don't know where you are?"

"I never do."

"Is it that hectic on the road?"

"I feel wanted, dead or alive. That old Bon Jovi song just hit me. Kinda like that."

"Mark sent me your itinerary for a stay at a resort in the mountains. It looks very quaint. I also like how he added bonus protection for you that looks like a Seal Team unit. I have their identification, everything."

"Yeah, there are some stationed in here, the shop next door, and down the street in a black van. I told them no white vans. I'm still creeped out by that last attack. Jasper's here with me, so that gives me comfort."

It was almost as if Jasper could hear her from five tables over. He glanced at her and winked. Her bodyguard might have her wired without even knowing it. She wouldn't doubt it.

"Any more threats, dear?"

"Here and there. Comes with it, I guess." Mary felt her spirit heavy-burdened and paused to pray.

"What was that?"

Mary picked up her menu to avoid her eyes. "What?"

"What you just did? It looked like you were praying."

"And, what if I was?"

"In public? There's bound to be paparazzi around here. They'll figure you're here soon enough if not already. They'll think you're muttering nonsense to yourself and have you pegged for going unhinged."

"I was praying, Lydia. That's all. I need for us to change the subject. The reason why I have you here is that we need to discuss a new manager position."

Lydia proposed something quick off the draw, like she'd planned it already. "Why not hire Mark?"

"That was fast."

"Why not? He's been with us for five years. He practically grew up with you. I believe he's someone you can trust, and after what you told me about the verbal garbage you've been collecting with Merv, I understand we need to remove any possibilities of that happening again."

"Who's Merv? I'm talking about Riff."

"I'm talking about Merv. That's the fool's real name. Merv Hammock. Lazy bum needs to go get stuck in a hammock and rock away the rest of his days between some jungle trees."

"That can't be his name."

"Well, it is. I make sure his payments are in order, and he sure doesn't get his checks delivered in the name of Riff. No bank would cash them."

"Oh, my goodness. His name is Merv? I can't. I just can't." And she couldn't stop laughing, and Lydia joined her.

Mark came over to the table and leaned in as Mary wiped the tears from her eyes. "Can you ladies cut it out? I can hear ye hooting like owls clear across to the other room. Ye're causing a scene if I ever saw one, and I thought ye wanted to lay low tonight."

"Did you know Riff's name was Merv?"

"Say again?"

Mary tried to repeat it, but she fanned for Lydia to do it. She couldn't catch her breath.

"Mr. Fired is actually not Riff at all, but his real name is Merv Hammock. There. I said it. Please don't make me say it again."

Mark joined in on their laughter.

The waiter came over and coughed. "Is there anything I can get for you ladies? Gentleman?"

Mary said, "Might as well sit down, Mark. We've got some celebrating to do, and it's all about you."

They ordered their food, and then Mark started in on the storytelling.

"You guys are getting me all nostalgic, and with this time of year, too, I might start to feel something."

Mark said, "It's okay to feel, Mary."

"Not really. When you feel, it hurts."

Lydia added, "But you also feel the joy mixed in with the hurt. You can't always control what feeling comes to visit, but you can be the one to allow it to stay the longest. Which one is taking up the most residence in your head?"

"Bitterness," she said, without thinking.

It just came out. She was bitter. For God taking her dad. For her mom being stupid over money and running away to not face what was happening.

"Forgive them," Lydia advised. "It's not worth holding all of this in, Mary. Besides, the lawyers guarantee a final resolution at the beginning of the year. It's not looking good for them, Mary. Due justice will be served."

Mary knew Lydia meant her mother and the Mitch character – a bodybuilding, steroid bottle walking. She probably hadn't figured out that she and God were in a rocky relationship, and she needed to find a way to work that out more than her forgiveness of her mother. She would rather make like her mother didn't exist. That was the easiest way to cope. It was harder to make like God wasn't there, when lately her spirit had been stirring in ways she'd forgotten about.

It all started with Josey Wales.

Her purpose had become so clear to her, and she could almost envision a new life ahead. Because of a child. One small act impacting Mary in ways she'd never thought for herself.

Mary blurted out, "Do you go to church?"

Lydia smiled. "I watch it online. Did you know that it's available to you even when you're on the road? I grew up in the church, homeschooled, all the like."

"I didn't know that," said Mark. "My uncle was a pastor of our little church back home, which meant my daddy always served on the deacon board. I was in the choir, myself. Just saying Mary isn't the only one with talent around here."

He started to bellow out in a frog voice, and Mary quickly clapped his mouth closed. Lovingly, but closed.

"So, you both have religious backgrounds. That's good to know. Another check off the list."

Mark said, "What list? I make the lists around here, and I haven't seen one with God on it, ever."

Mary had an idea. She could play matchmaker.

"And no husband, Lydia? Not yet?"

Lydia frowned. "What are you up to, Mary?"

"Never mind. Besides, let's make a toast to Merv."

Mark laughed. "Ye brought the name between us again? How am I supposed to drink my water after that without spewing? Stop making me laugh."

"Goodbye Merv, hello Mark."

"Hello? I'm right here."

"Exactly. Right where I want you to be. By my side, wherever this life takes me."

A puzzled expression crossed his face. "What am I missing here? What's going on?"

"You've just become Mary's new manager," announced Lydia. "That is, if you want the job. We never once considered you'd say no."

"Because ye knew I wouldn't. I'd be honored to be yer manager, Mary. I'm sure I can now start making manager lists. Piece of cake."

The waiter was walking by. "Would you like éclair or lemon cream?"

Mark turned to him and smiled. "Now that he mentions it, let's have dessert, ladies. Éclair for me."

Mary grinned. "He might need a thicker notebook. Maybe two. Lydia, order him four while you're at it. One for every season."

"Now that I'm yer manager, I'll be taking a lot better care of ye and the band, and the crew. Don't think that means we'll be kicking it up a notch in the new year, but actually going a little bit slower. Intentional. That's the word."

Lydia said, "I like intentional. It's with purpose. Clarity. It's not just a cacophony of clashing symbols."

"This woman is speaking my language. Purpose, Mary. Let's start doing things with purpose."

Mary said, "Things that matter."

"Like the other night. Did you see the positive headlines you received with the young girl from Make-A-Dream Organization? That's your first taste of using your fame for good." Lydia held out her phone and scrolled through the pictures. "I'm saving this clip on my phone forever of her singing. She was a doll."

Mary squeezed Mark's hand across the table. "Thanks for setting that up for me. It was something I needed that I didn't even know I did."

"Funny how giving back like that does good for the soul. It's been three years, Mary. It's time to honor him in these ways. As simple as that might have been for ye, it was mighty special for that little girl and her family. It was downright precious. I was very proud of ye."

"I was proud of myself. I don't know what prompted me to ask her to sing. It could have ended in disaster. It just felt right."

Mark said, "It wasn't on the list."

Lydia smirked, leaning over closer to Mark. "Maybe you need to get rid of the list?"

He joked, "I wouldn't dare hear of it. Has this woman lost her mind?"

Mary said, "I have an idea, and it's not on the list. Why don't you and Mark join me for the first couple of days at the resort. I really would like to share something with you guys, and it needs to be away from ears. I'm still trying to work it out all out in my heart, and like biscuit dough rising, it won't stay hidden for long."

"We could write in secret code. I could get us some invisible ink."

"I'm serious, Mark."

"I am, too. I've always wanted to be like George Washington's spies."

"Let's not get carried away. Lydia, do you have plans for Christmas?"

"Other than meeting with your songwriter to get new tracks for you for the new year, nothing much."

"You'll be working over Christmas?"

"It was actually convenient that I fly here. We've never met in person, only through phone conferencing and video. He lives here in North Carolina. He's ecstatic 'We Just Met, You Better Watch Out' made the final nomination list for Song of the Year. That's huge for his career as an artist."

"What's his name again?"

"You don't know?"

"It's not like I've talked to him. I just sang the song."

"It's more than just the song. He writes all of your songs. He is your personal songwriter. He's been the only one writing your songs since your rock stardom hit solid."

"And why didn't I know this?"

"You never asked," said Mark. "Besides, he's probably some old fogy wearing overalls named Cotton-Eyed Joe."

"It's better than Merv."

"Here we go again. Are we going to keep bringing this up?"

"Now that I know, probably the rest of my life."

Lydia said, "I should've told you his real name years ago if it brought you this much happiness. It's good to see you smiling."

"What's brought me happiness is the three of us together. I really need this, guys. Please promise me you'll stay a couple of days with me before you take off back to your own worlds. I don't want to be alone at Christmas."

The words must've hit both of their hearts at the very same time because their hands extended and fell on hers.

Mary laughed, "What is this? A new handshake?"

"I think managers can ask for secret handshakes and invisible ink."

"Don't start making demands. It hasn't even been ten minutes."

"True. I'll wait another twenty."

Lydia smiled. "You really do have a great sense of humor."

Mark gave her a dashing grin. "I think I do okay, for an old guy."

"And how old are you again, Mark? And you, Lydia?"

Mark cut in. "Don't ask her age, girl. Don't you know that's the first way to make a woman mad."

Lydia smiled. "Very true. I wouldn't reveal it in person or with invisible ink. Keep guessing, Mark."

Funny that Mark wasn't the one that asked it, but the play was already set in motion. Mary saw the way Lydia lit up each time Mark was just being Mark, and even though Mark was oblivious to it all tonight, she knew he was very intelligent. He'd figure it out soon enough.

"Then it's all settled," announced Mark. He motioned for a couple of guys to follow them. He'd had his security positioned and ready to leave at demand. "It looks like ye ladies will have to put up with me for a couple of days. Let me call my mother and tell her I'll be arriving later than scheduled."

"Will she be upset with you, Markie?"

"Don't call me that in public. She's used to it. She'll be so happy I got a promotion. It'll come in handy for them. Wait. Does that promotion mean a raise? No more late-night latte runs?"

"Raise, yes, but you do make the best salted caramel lattes when everything is closed, so maybe you can help a girl out in that department just out of the goodness of your heart. Lydia, set him up with a fair deal. Mark works hard. He deserves to be paid twice as much as you were paying Merv."

"I'll see to all of that, Mary. No worries. Is it 'Markie' that you want your checks made out to?"

"Mark. Mark. Just plain Mark."

"Mark Mark? Your first and last name is Mark? I thought it was O'Connell."

Mary laughed. "No more stage names. His name is Mark O'Connell. He should be named Mark Make-A-List-And-Check-It-Twice O'Connell."

"He'd run out of room on the signature lines."

"Good point."

"Not funny, Mary. Let me stay the comedian around here."

"Okay, deal."

She looped arms between the two of them as they hit the brisk night air. The downtown streets of Raleigh were bursting with crowds. She could put a name to a place and realized her feet felt more planted on the brick pathway that took them down the lane. She felt a little more grounded to life.

Restaurants were in full swing, and Mary glanced in at the people going about their evening, smiling, laughing, and toasting. It all seemed so easy, a life away from the stage. She wondered how many of them felt they had a purpose. How many of them were living their best life? She'd wasted so much time, and she was ready to start living again…or for the first time, really.

Shoppers carried last-minute bags and were apologizing as they squeezed their way between the crowds of a street market. She heard polite talk and pleasantries. People were nice. Not with their heads stuck down following feet in front of them, but actually staring into the eyes of others. Was this a thing of the South or just the way people acted in the world? It didn't feel like Hollywood at all. That was for sure.

She stepped from in-between Mark and Lydia and pushed the two of them together as she reached for a light-up bulb necklace, placing it around her neck and paying the merchant.

"I think it's time to get into the Christmas spirit."

"It matches your elf socks."

"I wear these all the time, not just the holidays."

"I know. So does half the world. How many pictures have you had accidentally wearing those blessed things?"

"They are blessed. Holy." She laughed at her own joke. They had a couple of worn places in them from wearing them over the years. The socks were one of the last gifts her dad got her before he passed away from leukemia, but she wouldn't tell them that. Some things were better left unsaid.

Others weren't. Like love between two unlikely people. That should be said. She just had to make them fall for each other first.

It's Him?

H is name is Presley Whitley. He'll be arriving soon. He's stuck down the mountain at some sleigh holdup."

Mary asked, "You mean a sleigh crash?"

Mark held up his local news feed flashing on his phone. "Apparently a Santa got robbed."

Lydia said, "Seriously? What's wrong with people?"

Mary shook her head. "The world's gone crazy. We've got the Seal Team in place, I see."

"Ready as always, just in case."

"You worry too much."

"And you don't worry enough. Didn't you just say the world's gone crazy."

"It has."

"Then trust me, I feel better with the security we have."

"I guess it's the military in you coming out."

Lydia said, "I didn't know you were in the military?"

"Yeah, I served in the Army and did a tour in Iraqi Freedom with Danny. That's how I know this little singing shrimp here. Me and her dad go way back to basic training."

"Makes sense now."

"What does?"

"Oh, nothing," said Lydia. "I somehow missed that on your resume."

"What? That I'm retired Army?"

"Yeah, that."

"That's why I could work for chump change. It's extra income."

"Don't start bragging about your paycheck. We could lower our deal," joked Mary.

"You heard nothing I said. You heard absolutely nothing," he chanted as he waved his hands in front of her face.

Lydia interrupted their playfulness. "There's your songwriter now. I can't believe you guys have never met. He's such a part of your success. I've always said, without the right song, it's hard for a singer to make it. The songs this man writes are special. A phenomenal talent."

Mark agreed. "He must've had a lot of life experiences because the depth of them is beyond what the other songs are today on stream. He's probably got more spiderwebs than me."

Mary stood up from the leather couch and folded the bear blanket. She'd been relaxing by the large community fireplace in the resort, drinking hot chocolate and taking in the Christmas music.

Mary asked, "Where is he?"

"Right there. He's coming this way."

Mary followed Lydia's gaze and was confused. "Wait? Which one? The older couple? They're a writing team?"

"No, the guy your age, short cropped dark hair, eyes that look like a passing storm. That one. The one with the corded sweater and scarf."

Mary stood speechless, watching him approach. He wrote her songs? He wrote the line, *forever shatters to brilliance? Long way to go before I find a home?* Her mind played over her jukebox and wave upon wave. She couldn't put the lyrics to the man in front of her.

He leaned over to give Lydia a quick hug. "I'm a hugger. Hope you don't mind. It's nice to finally meet you in person."

His country talk reminded her of the way her daddy talked, and she wondered if he was from Robeson County, too? He didn't look Lumbee, but he had that certain way about him that reminded her of her people.

"It's him?"

Mark said, "She's a hugger, too, even if she doesn't know it yet. Go on, Mary. Give the man a hug. It's like Elf in person, with his Christmas scarf and all. I bet you still have on those socks."

Mary blushed and couldn't help herself. She wanted to joke back to Mark but lost her ability to form a coherent thought.

Lydia said, "Presley, meet Mary Oxendine. No stage names on vacation."

Mary didn't move. She watched the way his eyes darted between the three of them as if he were trying to figure out the relationship.

He shook Mark's hand first. "Nice to meet you, sir. It's an honor to meet you and your daughter in person."

"I'm her manager." He laughed. "I like the sound of that. First time I've played around with saying it. I used to be her personal assistant. Ask me anything about Mary, and I'll know it. We could have the Mary quiz show, and I'd be sure to win the big bucks."

"Speaking of bucks. There are tons of deer roaming the resort lands. I almost hit one coming in."

"Are you a hunter?"

"Yes, sir. My family has a ranch now, thanks to the hits and Mary here. Thanks for always accepting my songs. It's changed my life."

"It's him?"

Lydia said with an exasperated sigh, "Mary, really. Is that all you have to say?"

Mary bit her lip. She didn't know what to say.

Mark cut through the awkwardness. "She thought you were collecting more spiderwebs than me. Take it as a compliment."

Lydia asked him the getting-to-know-you questions while Mary took it all in. He lived a couple of hours south of Asheville and was looking forward to his stay.

Mary found her voice. "You're staying, too?"

Lydia said, "Yes. We need to get the new package together. It should take a couple of days. He didn't have any immediate plans for Christmas and planned on driving in to see his folks on Christmas morning, then coming back to finish up the paperwork."

"Oh," Mary said, frowning at the prospect of having another wheel to complicate things. She was going to try to play Cupid the next couple of days. If Presley were here, that would probably take Lydia's attention away to business.

"I can leave if you want me to. I don't have to stay," Presley said, as if he could read her mind.

"No, it's not that. It's fine. Sorry, I'm really not rude."

"You acted a little rude, Mary," said Mark.

"Well, I was shocked. I was expecting an…an…"

"An old guy named Cotton-Eyed Joe," answered Mark. "Don't mind her. She has a wild imagination."

"I have no such thing. I just thought…"

"Do you like your songs?"

"I love them."

"I'm glad. Then, I'm doing my job right."

Lydia said, "In fact, we need to celebrate. We get the news about Song of the Year tomorrow, and just being nominated is worth a party. Either way, it's just in time for an early Christmas present. I'm sure you're going to win this one, Presley. You almost had it with Remember When."

"I think that's still my all-time favorite of all the songs I've written."

"And all the ones I've sung."

It reminded her of her dad. When life was simple. When things mattered. She got lost in the thoughts of her lyrics while the small talk continued around her. She blocked it all out as the image of her father found his way to her again. He lived in a small, neatly wrapped box that she often kept closed and only unwrapped when she was alone. Now, in the middle of a morning, with noise rattling around her, she found herself slipping off the bow to peek inside as she sang the lyrics of Remember When to him in her mind.

Remember when
Life was simple then
Remember when we were
Running barefoot in the wind
Watching kites reach the sun
Picking up pieces that'd come undone
Was so much easier then
All we had was time
To sit around and dream about
The way it would all turn out
Remember when

She got an email alert on her phone and looked down to see a new message from an account she didn't recognize at first. She almost swiped to delete it when it dawned on her who the outlaw could be. It was from Josey Wales.

She stood up and said, "I need to go and take care of something."

Mark said, "Anything I need to be aware of?"

"No, it's good. It's all good."

Mary moved toward the fireplace and sat down on the edge of the brick to read the email away from prying eyes. Grayish-blue eyes that were like a passing storm. Lydia got that description right.

Dear Mary,

I can call you Mary, still, right? The day of the concert was outrageously cool! I never imagined I could sing like that in front of people. How many fans do you think were there? Momma said maybe twenty thousand, but I'm not sure about that. It felt like more like a million. As soon as I heard your voice right next to me, it was almost like I could feel heaven right there on the stage. It made me not scared anymore.

I've been feeling better since that night. I've got tons of Instagram hits on the video, and people keep messaging me asking for a record deal. Daddy thinks it's all a big scam and says not to open the messages. I'm tempted to because wouldn't it be a dream come true to sing my very own song? I write songs. Did I tell you that? Probably not, because you didn't even know I could sing.

OR DID YOU?

Momma said she didn't write it in the application for Make-A-Dream. Was it Emma? My best friend might have told you. Oh, well. It was a make a dream come true, for real. Thanks again for everything. I won't keep emailing you like crazy, I promise. We (me, Momma, and Daddy) just wanted to wish you a Merry Christmas and to let you know we've been praying for you.

Every night we add a prayer for you. It's turning out to be the same one. Momma asked me why I pray it, but I can't really understand why. It's just something that comes out. Daddy said there's some things in life we aren't meant to understand. I think this fits that category. Well, anyway, bye! Merry Christmas!

P.S. You're awesome, but I know you already know that!

Your Friend (not a fan, but a friend...isn't that cool),
Josey Wales

As strange as it might have been, Mary felt connected to the young girl and did consider her a friend. To know she was being prayed for made Mary's heart feel a warmth that could melt an ice cream factory. She needed to be prayed for. It was about time she faced her faith head on.

She thought, No more running from you, God. I'm ready.

Maybe she'd pull strength from a new friend like Josey. Maybe she'd finally open up to Mark and Lydia and tell them how she needed to sing a new song. Whatever it would be, she knew she'd have to pray to find the courage to face it. It wouldn't be easy. Nothing ever was.

She Likes You

Mary brushed the tears from her cheeks and felt a hand touch her shoulder. It made her jump almost clear out of her skin. Everyone was always reaching out to her, invading her space. Why had she thought a vacation would be any different?

"I'm sorry. I didn't mean to scare you. Are you okay?"

Mary looked up into the eyes of her songwriter, and she saw a softness there that moved her. He had the kind of face that was unassuming, yet handsome at the same time. If she were going through model headshots for a new dancer, he wouldn't have caught her attention, but here, with a kindness that spread through his smile and actually reached his eyes, it was more than any headshot could capture.

She waved her phone in the air at him as if he could read her mind. Somehow, she found it a little more difficult to talk around him, too. Maybe it was also the lack of human contact outside of her circle that was causing her to be tongue-tied.

"Oh, charades! I love this game. Drama? No battery on your phone, and you need to check your status so you're about to have a meltdown? Boyfriend problems? I saw the tabloids about your breakup. Sorry about that."

"I'm not, and that's not what this is. Here, you can read it if you want to."

"You just hand random strangers your phone? I could run."

"I think Lydia has your information. We could track you down."

"Oh, good point." He held up the phone at an angle. "I was trying to appear cool and aloof, but now I've got to pull these out. Didn't know I was going to be tested on the first day and have to read aloud."

He slipped on a pair of black-framed glasses, and his eyes didn't do the funny squint anymore. His shoulders even relaxed.

"And you need those to see?"

"Yeah."

"And you weren't going to wear them? So, you'd rather fumble around in the resort? What if you'd grabbed another woman's shoulder, thinking it was me? You know you can get arrested for that where I come from."

"You were a little blurry. Now, I see you just fine and..."

He dropped his head, and two patches of red appeared on his cheeks. Mary wondered if he was just about to compliment her but decided not to push it.

He read the email, and his smile radiated. It was as if he were truly appreciating her words. "That's a sweet girl, right there. She's a songwriter, too. After my own heart. I wish I could've met her. That's awesome you did that for her and are still willing to keep in touch with her."

"She was the one that was awesome. She said something to me that stuck with me."

"What was it?"

"It matters."

"What?"

"Names. Things. Life. It matters."

"I agree. Smart kid."

"Yeah, smarter than me, that's for sure."

"Don't get all down on yourself. You're pretty special yourself to give her your personal email like that, and your Mary Oxendine name. She knows your name, and so does her family, away from the lights and set. That matters to her, I'm sure."

"You knew my name?"

"Lydia introduced us, remember?"

She didn't. She was more interested in the way the light was reflecting in the pools of his eyes, and in sizing up his boyish stance.

He broke through her thoughts. "It's on your personal email account. I am holding your phone."

"Next you'll want my I.D."

"I don't need it now. I have your name. I could look up everything about you if I wanted to."

"Are you a stalker or a fan, or a stalkerish fan?"

"I'm pretty sure I'm past that description."

"Which one?"

"The fan part. I'm not a stalker, if that's what you mean."

"Yeah, we can't be having any of that. So, you aren't a fan?"

"No."

"Now that's weird."

"I wouldn't call myself a fan. I write for you. It's more of a personal thing. You have a special quality about your voice, a unique tone."

"So I've been told."

"And that way you have fits with the way I write. I couldn't sing my own songs. It doesn't work that way."

"How does it work when you don't know me."

"I've searched up more than you know, and now that I know you as Mary Oxendine…the knowledge is just an enter key away."

"You could just straight up ask me questions. I wouldn't lie."

"Why? Aren't you used to putting on the stage front all the time? How would I know if it were Mary Bella or Mary Oxendine I was talking to?"

"I'm not on the stage when I'm with my people. You've been my songwriter for how many years now?"

"Going on a few."

Mary did blush, then, embarrassed a little that she hadn't spent the time to thank her songwriter for all of her hits. She didn't know his name and never bothered to even question where the lyrics came from. She just received the tracks in the mail, recorded the demo sessions, and made the final cuts in a day. She did feel as if every song had something pulled from her soul and placed into lyrics. Funny, they'd never met but she felt like he already knew her. She knew nothing about him.

"How did you get so talented?"

"You mean writing songs or knowing how to write for you?"

"Both, maybe."

"I've followed your career since you started."

"You sound like such an old soul. I followed your career…"

"I did. I'm only twenty-three. Don't get any ideas that I'm too old or too young or whatever that even means. No one is ever too young to do what counts. Writing music counts."

"And I've met another person in a month that walks around speaking quotes on a roll off the tongue without a blink. Like that's how people talk. Not to mention with the country slang from back home. It's almost like I'm stepping back in time before this life happened."

"First the girl jokes about my age, then she cracks on the way I talk." She noticed he was talking above her head and not to her.

Mark's voice was soft. "When she kids ye, she likes ye. Plain and simple as that. She likes ye well enough, then."

Lydia looked so cute standing beside Mark. His six foot four being towered over her small frame of five foot two. Mary stood up, just a little over Lydia's head, and turned to her with a silent plea to break the awkwardness Mark had created, but Lydia was blushing right along with her. Had they been making jokes back and forth? If they did, she took that as a sign he'd figured out her secret crush. Was it Mark with the crush?

Lydia grabbed Presley's elbow and led him back to the couch. "So, about the songs. We've got to discuss business before this storm rolls in. It looks like it could be a doozie."

The whole word like could be misconstrued supersonic fast down a road she wasn't ready to travel. She watched the snow steadily falling from the floor-to-ceiling paned windows beside the fireplace. It looked so tranquil out with the blanket of snow forming along the ridge line. Could it quiet the noise in her if she stood in it awhile?

"What's wrong, Mary?"

Mark knew her moods most days. She found herself more emotional than she'd been in a long time, after Josey. Maybe it was thoughts about her dad. Maybe it was seeing everyone happy and smiling during the holidays. Something was still missing from her life, and she couldn't name it. Well, maybe she could, but not aloud.

"It's hard to say. I shouldn't be complaining, right? Since this girl has everything."

"Just because ye have everything money can buy doesn't mean you have everything ye need."

"All these spoutings of wisdom. Maybe people do talk this way, and I've just never listened."

"I think ye're starting to notice."

"You told me that before."

"Ah, ye remembered. I've been worried about ye, Mary, if I must say so myself."

"Worried when you became my manager or worried when you were my assistant?"

"The worrying has never stopped. Ye're a sweet girl but ye put on this act of being all tough and hard as nails."

"Don't you think that's needed in this business?"

"Maybe a little, but I'm talking about the business of life. Ye don't let yer guard down even for a minute. When do ye catch yer breath?"

"I'm barely breathing now, it seems. Most days it's just me in a trance."

"Then, we need to get ye out of this funk ye're in and have some old-fashioned fun." He pointed to the snow. "Let's go make snow angels."

"I haven't done that in years, Mark. You know we didn't get much snow in Rob Co."

"Well, we won't discuss the amount of snow I've dealt with in Massachusetts. Besides, I haven't played in the snow in years, either. It might be fun."

"Mark? Having fun? Without a list?"

"That fine little lady over there did tell me to drop the list. Let's see if she'll take us up on the offer."

"Us? What if I pass?"

"You won't. Come on."

He grabbed Mary's hands and spun her towards Lydia and Presley who were having the lean-in conversation, the one that meant serious talk was occurring. She couldn't help but smile as Mark made the exaggerated announcement of having a snow day celebration, and why they shouldn't stay cooped up inside.

"That's the point," Mary said. "The fire. Warmth. Blankets. Look, they have a coffee bar."

"That can wait, Mary. Let's go have some fun."

Lydia frowned. "But we have business."

"That we can discuss over dinner." He grabbed her hands and pulled her off the couch. "I think snow angels are in order."

"I've seen those on television movies."

Mark put his hand over his heart, a reference to The Jeffersons sitcom. Mary wondered if Lydia had ever watched the reruns. Mark was a unique somebody, that she prayed Lydia would want to learn more about. The more Mary watched their looks, the more she started to see it burning from the both of them. A resort cabin in a picturesque setting surrounded by thousands of twinkling lights and Christmas decorations might lighten all their moods.

The light was there. The connection was growing. Mary could sense it.

Mark acted wounded. "Ye've never made snow angels?"

"I'm from Los Angeles. We don't get snow."

"But it's the City of Angels, and I always wondered why it was called that. It makes perfect sense to me now."

Mary hid a laugh. That was a full-on old man pick-up line. The big flirt. Go, Mark, she thought.

Presley said, "Look, they have suits we can rent. We won't even get your designer outfit messed up."

Mark clapped. "It's all taken care of, then. No excuses allowed, ladies. Hold on."

Mary watched as Mark headed over to the counter. Before long, he was carrying back four suits. "They even had yer favorite color, Mary."

"How thoughtful of them," Mary said, smirking as she held up the suit next to her, already figuring it would swallow her whole. "And does that make me want to put this Eskimo suit on?"

"It will protect ye from feeling the wet and cold effects of all that. Ye'll thank me for it." He pointed through the glass, and the snow was swirling like magic.

Mary grabbed the suit and boots from Mark. She realized he wasn't going to take no for an answer. She needed forced fun because at the moment, if she would have stayed inside, she would've been brooding. She didn't want that, either. She lived in the middle of gray and blurred lines, and decided she needed more of the right way. A step away from what didn't make sense to her anymore. Mary prayed for more color in her life. Even if that color were white snow.

The others went to grab their boots. Mark knew her size, and practically everything about her. She wondered if he could pick up her strange emotions as she watched how easily Presley was laughing with Lydia at the counter. Maybe he could write her a list on how to feel.

"He's nice, Mary. A regular guy."

"Regular? There's a kind? Like no flavored syrup, cream, or sugar?"

"He's not a coffee ye can order up. He's just a guy walking towards a girl. That's it. Simple. Ye need a guy like that."

So, he did have a name for what she was feeling. "I don't need a guy, period. Look how touring and relationships don't work. We start off a grand New Year kick-off, right?"

"Remember when I told ye I was going to force ye to go a little slower next year? Ye've got to make time for what's important. Well, in yer case, I think ye need to figure out what's important, and then spend time in it. Doing it. Living it. Whatever."

"I thought riding the wave of the fandom while it lasted was the most important focus we could take. My fifteen minutes of fame might be ending soon. The next Mary Bella is waiting in the wings."

"Ye've had a long shelf life already, and one reason is because ye sing ye're heart out to people, across ages. It's a timeless thing ye do. Trust me, ye're just getting started. Ye're not a one hit wonder, Mary."

Lydia chimed in, nudging Presley in the arm. "Thanks to him. With his lyrics and your voice, it's like pure magic happening. And to think, you've never talked. I just assumed the both of you kept in touch. It's like he knows you, Mary."

"I was thinking the same thing," said Mary, before realizing she shouldn't have said it aloud. She didn't need to divulge anything of what she was thinking. Especially how fine Presley looked with the black suit now zipped up around him, making his eyes pop even more.

Presley said, "Well, I do know her email now, so I think maybe we could write now and then. It would keep me in the Mary loop."

"The loop of no return," she said. "It's a round and round, never-ending dance move."

"That sounds awful." He grimaced. "I can write, not dance. Don't even ask me to do that, Mark. Snow angels, easy. I can look ridiculous like a duck flapping its wings. Dancing? No way. Not in this lifetime."

Mary laughed. "Be careful what you say around this guy. He'll find ways to make you dance, Presley."

Lydia said, "I'll remember that. I can't dance, either."

"Then it's settled. Dance lessons tonight at nine."

"A date with a book tonight at nine," corrected Lydia.

Mark and Lydia walked in front of Mary and she could overhear them discussing Tolkien and Vince Flynn. Two unlikely author names mixing right together in a lively conversation.

Presley said, "I like them."

"I love them. They're my people. The two I have left."

"No family?"

"No."

She wasn't going to talk about her mother with him. If he'd followed her career, he was sure to know the scandal of a mother she didn't claim anymore.

"I have four older brothers, who are over-the-top loud and obnoxious. They're my best friends, pretty much. Three of us still live together. My oldest brother, Daniel, he ran off this year and got married. I'll be an uncle in the new year. Crazy."

Mary thought he must be the quiet one of his clan. The songwriter who sat alone with a journal, making rhymes and daydreaming. He didn't seem the over-the-top kind.

Mark was the first to spread out his arms like he was about to take off and fall against the snow. "And ye do this, and do this some more, and one more time, and..."

He stood up and jumped out of the snow angel with an exaggerated hop. He seemed proud of his first attempt.

"It's that easy?" asked Lydia. "I think I can manage that."

"You can't mess a snow angel up. It's impossible."

Lydia fell beside Mark's pattern and made her print in the snow. Side by side the angels looked like an oversized and miniature version of a thing closely resembling angels if the head was angled sideways and maybe had a squinty eye. Mark snapped a picture of the patterns.

Lydia tried to brush the snow from her suit and took two steps back when Mark came to help. "At least you didn't snap a picture of me while I was looking ridiculous in the snow flapping my arms."

"You had your eyes closed. I just might have a picture right here."

Mary smiled at them as they chased one another in the snow, like two children ready for a snow fight. Mark was always one to kid around, but this time, she was sure he was having a wonderful time doing it. She leaned against a tall oak and watched the scene play out.

"I feel like I'm in some kind of movie. Trapped here as the world keeps spinning, but right now, everything feels like it's stopping. It's disorienting." She held out her hand to catch the snow. It was falling fast and collecting against the padding of the suit.

Presley said, "They're cute." He motioned to Lydia and Mark. Lydia hit Mark square with a snowball. For a California girl, she had it down pat in no time. Then, she felt Presley's body shifting closer.

He looked down at her and brushed snow off her cheek. "You're cute."

"Cute? That sounds like you think I'm twelve. That girl is cute doesn't mean pretty or hot or gorgeous. She's just cute."

"But you are. I don't want to think of you as hot. It doesn't fit. You're adorable, Mary." She recognized his shyness creeping in. It pooled right below his eyes in patches of red. "There's so much I want to say to you."

"And you just met me. You don't know the power of my dark side."

"That can't describe you. I won't allow it. There's power in words we speak."

"I can be quick tempered. Which might be a goal to work on for the new year. I'm always looking for a challenging resolution I'll never master."

"He that is slow to anger is better than the mighty; and he that ruleth his spirit than he that taketh a city. Proverbs speaks what you need to say into your life, and the Spirit will take care of the rest."

"So, you're quoting the Bible now? I've never met a guy who did that."

"And that's a shame. You've been meeting the wrong kind of guys."

"Apparently."

"Do you believe in God, Mary? That's something I don't know about you. Nothing in your biographies or interviews ever mentions your faith."

"I know. We have to keep it that way. It could ruin my fan base and alienate me, pretty much ruining everything we've tried to build. But I believe in God. God and I have a sticky relationship going on right now. Sometimes I stick to Him, and then other times I feel myself slipping from His grasp, like my adhesive wears off, and I move further away no matter how hard I try to stay stuck."

She put her hand over her mouth and looked around in horror.

"What's wrong?"

"I can't believe I said all of that. Are you recording this conversation? Oh, no!"

"Mary, calm down. I'm not recording. Look. You can trust me. I'm not like Darian. Far from it." He unzipped his snowsuit and pulled his phone out of his pocket. It was off.

He was referring to her ex who'd caught her badmouthing the press on his voice memo without her knowledge, and he'd exposed her as soon as the breakup hit the newsstands. She was in a lawsuit now because of it over defamation of character. All because she thought she could trust him enough to speak her mind around him, and she did let her anger get the best of her when she was around Darian. Something about him fueled a negative energy, the same way Riff did. She was glad both of them were out of her life for good.

She tried to calm her nerves and get her mind off the venom that had sickened her for too long. "Any more Bible verses you can throw out there for me that might be useful?"

"Love bears all things, believes all things, hopes all things, endures all things. Love never ends."

She turned to watch Lydia and Mark now holding hands. That didn't take long, and she didn't have to do any matchmaking at all.

"Love? Have you ever been in love before?"

His country accent dropped like sweet honey when his voice went low. "I think I might be."

She noticed he was using present tense. Of course, he had a girlfriend, and she felt a sigh release. She couldn't start anything with the man in front of her. The tour would take her away, and she'd be left brokenhearted and alone again.

Mark called out, "It's your turn, Mary. Make an angel."

She moved away from Presley towards the laughing couple but thought she heard him whisper, you already are one.

Maybe it was the wind playing tricks on her. It had picked up considerably since they'd arrived.

Mary fell into the snow and was surprised when Presley was right beside her. She watched as his smile spread across his red cheeks, from the bitter cold or embarrassment, she wasn't sure which. It didn't matter that Mark was taking shots of them. She knew he wouldn't post it on the five o'clock news. Pictures that she could look at for days when snow would seem far away, and life would be complicated.

She needed the uncomplicated. Simple. Truths. And she felt a warmth fill her spirit, in the midst of a snowstorm.

She wouldn't allow any more negative thoughts to invade her mind. She'd try to make the moments count. No more anger, she spoke over her soul. No more bad choices. No more fear. She prayed, let me live in the light, Lord. Show me how. I need to learn how to love you and myself. Give me the strength to say to them what I need to say and not let this all fall apart in the end. Amen.

You Spin Me

Presley said, "Dinner was fantastic. I loved the strawberry and feta salad with raspberry vinaigrette. We don't have fancy stuff like this where I'm from. It's a Thousand Island kind of place."

"Nothing wrong with that, in fact, I know that Mary's favorite late night secret sauce comes from a place with golden arches," replied Mark. "I've enjoyed hearing about ye and the country lifestyle. It might be something I'd look into myself with retirement approaching in the next ten years. A ranch with a shooting range in North Carolina sounds nice."

"My daddy is a concealed carry instructor, among other things, like taking care of our cows."

Lydia said, "I've never been to a farm or shot a gun."

Mark dropped his fork and didn't care in the least it made a loud ding on the plate. "Seriously, lady? Ye don't dance. Ye've never milked a cow. Ye don't shoot. What is it that ye love to do?"

"Read."

"Quiet nights by a fire are ye're specialty, then?"

"I'm pretty good at it. Years of practice."

"Well, let me find you a book about shooting and dancing, and then I might be able to convince you to give it a try."

"All you'd have to do is ask, and I'd say yes."

Mark was the one blushing now. "Does that mean if I asked ye right now, ye'd say yes?"

"Maybe, if you ask me proper."

Mary didn't know what he was referring to, marriage or a date? With Mark, all bets were off. He might elope right there in the resort. He'd been silent about his love life for so long, Mary figured he was just low-key about it. Maybe he was waiting for the perfect woman. Maybe he knew all along who that perfect woman was, and Mary wasn't the one that was noticing.

Mary and Presley must have had the same thoughts because they both leaned in as if all they needed was a bucket of popcorn between them. They bumped shoulders and the shock startled Mary. Presley kept leaning in.

"Will ye, then?"

Lydia didn't blink or hesitate, she only whispered, "Yes."

"It's settled then," said Mark. "I'm asking this pretty lady to dance, and she already said yes."

Lydia smiled even though she started to make another excuse. "But there isn't a dance floor."

"There wasn't a canvas either, but that didn't stop Michelangelo from painting a masterpiece on the Sistine Chapel ceiling."

"It took him four years to paint his frescos. It might take me four years not to step on your toes. Don't say I didn't warn you."

Mark's eyes grew bright with playfulness. "Four years of practice time might not be enough. I don't mind if you do, actually. My feet are numb from the cold! I wouldn't feel a thing anyway."

Lydia and Mark left them at the table, their hands already connected as soon as they stood. Mary knew this was the making of a fine beginning for the two of them.

Presley asked, "Did that just feel like we were intruding on some private conversation in the middle of a first date?"

"Yes! I thought so, too. Even though it was awkward, it was the sweetest thing I've ever seen. I've never seen Mark so…"

"Smitten?"

"Is that the word for it?"

"Yeah, I think so. It's that old kind of love that comes once in a lifetime. The kind that knocks at your door and sits with you in your parlor for a little while, only wanting your presence and your hand to hold. That kind of innocence."

"And that was also something descriptive I wouldn't have expected from you either. Romantic and quoting the Bible."

"You are starting to get me, I guess." He stood up from the table and held out his hand to her.

Would she say yes? To whatever this was? A help up from a seat? A lacing of fingers? Palm-to-palm kissing?

Mary pulled back her chair and stood beside him without accepting his offer. It was awkward enough being out for so long without an entourage or attacks from fans that she was feeling a little too exposed.

She tried to change the subject to music. That was her way out of anything weird building up between them.

"I can't believe you've finished ten new tracks for me. Is it a theme this time? Is it a love album? You quoting love bears all things made me wonder if that's what might be inspiring you to write."

"It's a little different than I was hoping for. Maybe even a little darker than you've sung in the past. I'm concerned why they asked me to go that direction. I turned in what they wanted but that's really what I wanted to talk to Lydia about. It's not that the songs aren't ready. They are. I just don't think it's right for you. It's hard to stand by what I've written this time."

"Dark? Like how dark?"

"One in particular spirals. This Riff character must be trying to shape you into an edgier star."

"Riff is gone. Is that where the order came from?"

"Yes, he said you were also needing one for a beer endorsement, and it had to have a harder, rock edge to it."

"You turn twenty-one in the industry and new opportunities start to knock."

"Like beer commercials? With a polar bear and a zebra?"

"I didn't agree to it. I don't know why he asked you to do that."

"He said it was a done deal."

"There's no way I could sign those papers. I left them on his desk to collect dust. My dad battled with alcohol for a while after his tour and tried to drown out his PTSD with the hard stuff instead of seeking treatment. After he got sick, he stopped drinking, cold turkey, and made me promise to never touch the stuff. He wouldn't want me to advertise it, either. Young girls look up to me. They might think I'm trying to make it look cool. I can't have that on my conscience. I've made too many bad decisions already in my life. I can't add that to the mix."

"Then, it's settled. Let me drop that song. I won't show it to you."

"What if I told you a secret about my plans for…"

Mark interrupted them. "Why are ye two still talking over here? The floor is waiting."

Mary said, "There is no dance floor."

He stomped on the heart pine wood. "There is a floor. This is a dance." He did a couple of side steps. "It's officially a dance floor. Where's yer creative flow? Yer imagination?"

"Frozen from making snow angels and having snowball fights with you."

"Then, let's all dance together by the fire and get toasty."

"This is a Christmas song in the making," she said, as she followed Mark.

She turned and saw the look of horror on Presley's face. Mark saw it, too. "Come on. I've got Lydia dancing. I'll teach ye all the moves I know."

"Don't learn a single move from him. Trust me. He dances like a chicken."

She wished she hadn't have said it, because Mark didn't care who was witness, he started bawking and squawking and doing the chicken dance.

"Are you sure he didn't sneak something in his water? Like vodka? Something clear?"

"This is him sober. He doesn't drink, either. In honor of my dad."

"I'm sorry I didn't get a chance to meet your dad. He sounds like someone worth honoring."

Mary stopped walking. Her heart stopped along with her steps. "You had no right to say that."

"I'm sorry. I didn't mean to upset you."

"Mary, what's wrong?" Mark was there in a second, standing tall and alert.

"Nothing, Mark. I'm fine."

"When a woman says she's fine, she isn't fine, Presley. That's words of wisdom right there."

"I'll take that to heart," he replied.

"Come on, Mary. Whatever the boy said, I'm sure he didn't mean it by the look on his face. Give him some credit. He's a little awkward, and he looks a little goofy with that sideways grin, but he'll do."

Presley laughed. "Dag on, man. You tell it like it is, don't you?"

"Better not waste time saying it any other way."

"Then, I don't think the dance idea is a good idea for me. You think I'm awkward now. You ain't seen nothing yet."

"Why are you so adamant on dancing, Mark? There isn't any really good music playing for us to dance to."

"I can fix that. Let me see if I can tap into their playlist with mine."

"So, now you'll be demanding and make requests?"

"I can do it in a nice way. A wink and charm go a long way."

"I'll remember that, too," said Presley.

He tried to wink at Mary, and his squinted face made her smile. She realized he wasn't the kind she could stay mad at for long. Besides, his remark was innocent. She was the one being defensive and should be apologizing.

"I guess if you smile at me that way, I can't say no to a dance."

"It's no big deal," she said. "We don't have to. Let Mark try to play Mr. Romance. I might just go on up and see what's on. I haven't binge watched something in a long time. I bet I have hundreds of shows to catch up on."

"I don't watch a lot of television."

"No? What do you do to relax?"

"Take trail walks. Hunt. Shoot. Write songs. I'm working on a novel now, too. So, that's a new venture. It's about a guy who falls in love with a girl way out of his league. He doesn't know how it ends, though."

"You mean the guy or you? Aren't you the writer? Don't you have it all planned out?"

"No. I have no clue what's going to happen next. I'm just honoring the blank page in front of me and letting God help me figure out the rest."

"That sounds like a song lyric. Maybe that should be one we can work on together."

"About God? Me and you? Write a song?" He seemed surprised. "I didn't know you wrote lyrics."

Mark pointed to the corner speakers hanging by the fireplace. "They're about to play our song."

Lydia said, timidly walking towards him with her arm outstretched, "And what's that?"

"At Last, by Etta James. It's going to say all the words that won't come out right from me. I'll let her do all the romantic lines. We can just sway."

Presley said, "Is he trying or is that the natural Mark with the lines?"

"I think that's Mark. I've got a feeling he's being true to himself. I wish I could say all the things racing around in my head, but all the dust kicking from the tire tracks leave everything overcast."

"You can with me, Mary. I won't hurt you."

"Your eyes get overcast. They change from gray to blue like the line between a storm and a break in the clouds."

Did she just say that out loud to him? Was Mark's boldness creeping into her psyche and breaking her walls of resistance? Maybe it was the song. Maybe it was the crackling of the fire or the way Presley smelled when he stepped closer to her to put his arms around her waist. Hold it in, girl, she thought. Next, she'd be telling him that he was cute…handsome…hot….

"Sway? That's it? Oh, I could've done this a long time ago," he spoke too soon. He apologized for stepping on the side of her shoe.

"It's okay. You know you can spin me. This song reminds me of one of those black and white movies, where the leading man bowed to his girl and spun her around the dance floor."

"Don't be having those kinds of expectations of me or you might be let down. I'm no Fred Astaire. I can spin you once and pull you close."

"Fair enough," she whispered, feeling the warmth rise around her. His height made it easier for her to spin under his arm, and she found herself stepping closer than they were before.

"Mary, I…"

"Don't say anything. Let's listen to the lyrics. Let's see what Mark wants to tell Lydia."

They listened to the slow song speaking volumes as deep as an ocean. When it was over, a few of the late-night patrons clapped for them. Mary saw for the first time that an older couple had joined the dance hall party. That made her smile even more.

"If only I could write lines like that."

"You do a pretty good job, future Song of the Year winner."

"But that's a classic kind of song. One that matters so much to Mark that he played it for his dance with Lydia. I want my music to be that important to someone else years later when I'm gone."

"Your music is important, to me. Maybe you just need a live concert. Have you been to one of my concerts?"

"No, but maybe you can help me with that."

"I can't, Presley. I can't get involved with you if that's what you're trying to say. I can't do this." Mary ran from the room as the claps continued, and the next song began to play. Tears fell as she bounded up the staircase to her room.

She heard him call from the bottom of the staircase. "Wait, don't run away. I'm sorry, Mary."

Mary didn't turn around but was thankful he wasn't following her. He spun her more than in a circle. Her whole world and heart were on fire, and she felt like she was dancing in the flames. I'd be the one hurt, she screamed at herself. I'd be the one left.

Mary pushed aside her tears and started to run a bath. She grabbed her journal and wrote…

> If I don't get too close, then I can't get burned
> If I let him in, then I've never learned
> You spin me but I'm broken
> Skipping record lines and repeating being left behind
> Instead of whole you get me wounded
> And I'll never let you hold me again
> Never say never because if you were here
> Right now, right here
> I'd let you spin me again

Mary pushed her journal aside and thought, Save the song lyrics for Presley.

She just wouldn't leave her room. No, that wouldn't be handling her life, just locking herself away. She couldn't hide from the welling of emotion that pinged against her spirit like rain on a tin roof. And now with Mark as her manager, and Lydia and him practically on the verge of getting married, this might be her chance to break the news.

Are You Serious?

The knock on the door didn't surprise her. Every chance she had to be alone was always interrupted with some nonsense or another. She had just snuggled up with Stitch and found a new horror series on Netflix she was planning to watch all night.

Mary knew it wasn't Mark because he was probably still downstairs dancing with Lydia, oblivious to her escape. Her security detail was already in place. She heard them rustling outside and a couple of walkie-talkie beeps gave her some comfort she needed to settle in.

Another knock meant he wasn't going away.

One of the men barked through the door, "Miss, the boy left you a note."

Mary leaned against the frame. "Is he gone?"

"Yes, ma'am. I told him you didn't want to be disturbed."

"Thanks, Jasper. That is you, isn't it?"

"Yes, ma'am."

"Just slide it under the door."

"Yes, ma'am."

She wanted to say enough with the yes, ma'ams, but figured it came with the territory. Jasper had been her personal bodyguard from day one, and was her head of security, which was now close to twenty strong and growing since her fame had tripled during the past couple of years.

A note? What guy wrote notes? Apparently, romantic Bible-quoting songwriters wrote notes. His list was growing longer by the hour.

Dear Mary O.,

Not the Mary Bella I've been writing for, but for Mary O., the one I've been falling for. Seven is my lucky number. I've figured if I'm going to do this the right way, it has to come in sevens. Seven is the number of completion, and today I received my confirmation that you do complete me, heart and soul. I have to write you seven things on my mind. I don't know what they'll be yet, but I've been praying about this blank page. I figure God will help me with all the words I need to say. I hope you don't mind I've got Him involved in this because He is. Done. Right in the center of it.

I'm not good at this. Any of this. I've never had an "official" girlfriend before, and I know that might sound strange, but I'm too shy for all that. I couldn't approach a girl, let alone tell her I liked her. But I like you. I really like you.

I've been keeping around letters to you since I wrote your first song. Pick Me Up came with a letter you never received. Even if I had your email back then, I would've never sent it. It told you what I was thinking about while I was writing the song. It told about an awkward teenage boy with a crush on a superstar, who happened to land a lucky break with a song entry at a local contest at the radio station. The rest is history. I have a letter for every song if you want to read them.

You probably figured out music is my life. At Last made me want to write you this note. Holding you close was more than the rush of a final note of a completed song. You make sense to me. Something about you fits.

I want to know more about you. We don't have to rush anything. I just want to be your friend for starters. That's all. I promise. If we stay friends, then we do. If we become what I think we will, then we do. All I can do is leave it up to prayer and a promise I won't hurt you.

I won't hurt you. That deserves a line all on its own and I won't. I mean it. I won't.

I don't have a game. The roses are red, violets are blue kind of game is about all I've got. I'm not good at cards or movie trivia but you can believe what I say and know I mean it. I don't speak out of line and speak straight. It's hard for me to look at you and speak. I think that happened to you, and I don't know why. Whatever that was, down there, between us. I felt it strong, Mary. I think you did, too.

Give me a chance, Mary. I don't know what a chance even means between us. Does that mean you'll go out on a date with me if I ask you to? Maybe not.

Does it mean I'll ask you to be my girl, and you'll say yes? Maybe not. But a chance has to start with you not running away. Talk to me, Mary. Say you will.

Yours,

Presley

She let the paper fall on her blankets and put Stitch up to her chin, resting her head between his ears. It felt honest enough. It felt like he was right there in front of her, leaning in to brush the snow off her cheek.

She turned to her playlist. Music. Her brain needed a distraction while she willed her heart to calm the erratic beating. She hit shuffle and rolled her eyes.

"Seriously, God. You're going to go there?"

She leaned back on the pillow and brought his letter close to her for one more inspection. If only she could test it for validity. That would take more than invisible ink.

An old one by Rascal Flatts, God Blessed the Broken Road, hit the chorus by the time she read it through, and she couldn't help but sing along. If they had a song, this would have to be it. She'd tell him about how it was the first to play when she read his letter.

She switched it off and sat up, pushing the covers aside. What was she thinking? She'd do no such thing. They wouldn't have a song because they wouldn't be. He just needed new material and was using her to try to stir up some emotions. She cracked open the door, the note pressed against her. She looked down the hallway and saw it was clear.

"Do you know his room number?"

"We know every person in and out of this entire establishment, Mary. We even know the owners and their two dogs, when they bought the place and for how much. That's what we do."

"Can you escort me, then?"

"Yes, ma'am."

She folded the note and slipped it into the pocket of her pajamas. His was the number seven to her nine. Two doors down. It reminded her of an old Dolly Parton song her parents used to sing on vacation trips.

She knocked and said, "Don't open the door. I'm in my pajamas."

"And does that mean you're walking around exposing yourself in the hallway? I think that you should know by now that…"

"Open the door."

He laughed and did as she said. "I love your Stitch pajamas."

"Are you serious? Is this a game you're playing? Some new story you're writing and trying to get a new main character down with a top seven list of winning traits no one would ever believe to be real? Romance. Bible memorization. Love letters. What's next? You gonna ask me for a walk in the stars and say you'll capture one for me in the palm of your hand?"

"First, I am serious. You aren't in my novel, not yet anyway. But let me go write that star part down before I forget. That would actually be a good line. I'll capture stars for you, see. In the palm of my hand, see." He rasped his voice, then held out his hand to her in a dramatic flair.

"I can't do this with you, Presley."

"Do what? Have a conversation in pajamas? Then get dressed. We'll go down and get a hot chocolate."

"This." She handed him back his note. "Take it, please. It would hurt me to keep it."

"It hurts me to take it."

"Then we're already hurt. The both of us. We did a mighty fine job at messing it up before it could begin. No drawn-out disaster in the making. Because I'm sure that's all it could ever be. Clean breaks are best."

"I don't want a break. I want glue."

"I'm not gluing myself to anyone or anything right now."

"If it's a clean break, I can at least get a cast on my arm. You can sign it. You're used to handing out autographs."

"You're making no sense right now."

"Neither are you. Saying we'll be a disaster when I have insider knowledge, we'd be just the opposite."

"You need to get over yourself."

"I need caffeine right now. You don't believe me. Chocolate has caffeine."

"It's late. You shouldn't drink caffeine."

"And you shouldn't give back love letters. That's rude. You're pushing me away and giving me health advice in the next breath. I'm trying to understand you, Mary. Let me know you."

Jasper said, "He's right, you know. That was kind of low, Mary."

She gasped. "Jasper. I didn't know you were listening."

"Um…really? I listen to everything. And this guy is legit."

"And how do you know this?"

"I told you I know everyone in this resort. Besides, he's the one that's been feeding the songs to keep this show alive. I've known about him for the last five years, and within the last fifteen minutes with that love letter…I might need you to help me with a little surprise Christmas present for my wife."

Presley said, "Hey, I'm standing here. What's going on?"

"He's my bodyguard. Meet Jasper."

"I didn't even see you there. Has he been there the whole time?"

Jasper stepped from around the edge of the hallway corner and shook Presley's hand. "He has a firm handshake. Not slimy. Good sign."

"And what do you know about me again?"

"Your address, number, cell, email, high school transcripts, where you went to college, how you can hit a target dead center, and about the time when you fell off the second floor of the barn and …"

"That's enough. I believe you."

"What happened at the barn?"

"Hot chocolate?"

"No. Never mind. I don't care. You probably broke something, talking about casts. You've had experience."

"Not enough with rock stars, apparently. I don't know what's the deal with you. You aren't like this, Mary."

"Like what?"

"All tough and with these nasty comebacks. You sound like you're trying to be mean but it's all a front. You're wearing Stitch pajamas. How am I to take you seriously in those?"

"And now you have something against Stitch?"

"No way, I love Stitch. It's not that. I'm just trying to tell you that it's okay to like me."

"I don't like you."

Jasper said, "I think she likes you a little too much, or we wouldn't be standing here doing this."

"We...I pay you to watch out for me, not get me into trouble."

Jasper sighed. "I'm trying to save you from yourself, Mary. Sometimes that's the strongest enemy you'll ever face, real or imagined."

Mary turned and walked back toward her room. It was hopeless. She wasn't going to continue to engage with Presley Whitley. Period. She'd talk to him through Lydia. That had worked fine all the years prior to their meeting.

That was the first thing she'd get straight in the morning. She made a dramatic entry back into bed and pulled the covers over her head.

No.

More.

Presley.

When they found out her decision, there might not be any more Presley anyway. That would solve it all. Another reason to follow her heart. To lead herself away from a guy who would be bound to hurt her and follow the way her spirit was calling her to go.

I Can Do This

For the first time in years, Mary ordered her own latte without Mark standing beside her or serving her. Jasper and the men were positioned casually in the open resort room, one reading the newspaper, another sketching a scene in his art pad, but all with their eyes on her and their surroundings.

She was just settling in herself, finding it nice to take in ordinary people going about their morning on their vacations. Children were standing in awe in front of the Christmas tree that reached to the ceiling, marveling at the lights and ornaments.

Mary fell in love at first sight with the English bulldog that sauntered next to her, head flopping side to side with a kind of happiness that could only be found with paws. Mary had never seen a dog so cute. He was dressed in a Santa sweater. She asked the owner if she could take a picture.

The lady gladly obliged, and Mary took a snapshot of the puppy, who was not being camera shy at all and decided to roll over as soon as she started snapping.

"What's your dog's name?"

"Rambo. You know, after the movie series with Sylvester Stallone. He just turned a year old this week, the best Christmas gift I've ever received. Do you have any pets?"

"I can't. I'm always on the road and..."

"Oh, I hear you. Traveling for business gets old pretty quick. I was once a pharmaceutical sales rep, so I understand your pain. I was all over the country. That was for the birds, I tell you. Now, I'm back in school to get my teaching degree."

"Good for you," Mary said, thankful she hadn't spilled anything about her tour schedule or leaked who she was.

She didn't need the press knowing her whereabouts. They'd have a field day with her being seen with Presley and peg him as her new love interest. The way he looked at her last night when she gave him back his love letter let her know the paparazzi wouldn't have to stretch the story too far to make this one believable, just get a picture and let the analysis begin. They'd take it to the bank, for sure.

Mary was too relaxed, sipping her latte, in her faded jeans and Goonies sweatshirt. She couldn't afford to get too comfortable. The stranger went on about her morning with her dog, leaving her time to start creating her own mental list of all the wrongs she'd done in the past few years. She had enough for at least seven mistakes to get her started. Why not? If it were lucky maybe it could help her erase everything.

First thing on the list was not having enough time to get a dog, but the worst of it would be the extreme mistake of her father passing away while she was on tour and she didn't get to say goodbye, to the time when she busted the hotel television with her guitar or smashed the set of her hair commercial because they wouldn't oblige her. Before she could continue to let the guilt take over her again, Mary saw Mark and Lydia walking downstairs together, with Presley in tow.

What did they do, plan an intervention? Synchronize their watches?

She didn't rise but addressed Lydia first. "May I have a word with you," she said as she glanced between the guys. "Alone."

Presley smiled at her, and her sadness suddenly washed over her like water, churning buttery emotions she didn't even know she had.

She turned from him and stared into the crackling fire as he spoke, feeling as if her very heart was sitting among the wood and coals. "She wants to say she's not talking to me. But she's technically talking to the air around me, so I think that counts."

The tension around them was thick, like they all came to her with a rain cloud in the forecast. They'd definitely been conspiring upstairs by the way they kept exchanging looks.

Mark tried to change the subject. "I see you got your coffee this morning."

He was used to diffusing situations. He'd had enough experience at it. Poor Mark. She needed to apologize to him. He didn't deserve the way she'd acted.

Lord, forgive me, she whispered. "Very observant, Mark. Yes, I did and managed just fine."

"Managed…manager…I've got eyes on ye, Mary. Ye've got talent. I've always said it."

"Okay, we need to talk, too, I guess. Just me and you and Lydia. Let's just leave this guy here to his own business, whatever it is he's doing, and let's go get some breakfast somewhere, anywhere, away from here."

Mark said, "How about we go nowhere. The road coming in and out of the place is closed temporarily."

Lydia said, "I've never seen so much snow in my life."

"Neither have I," answered Presley. "I think we'll be here a couple more days."

Mark said, "That means we'll need to break it to my parents that we're missing a holiday again because of…"

"Me. I know. Add to my guilt I was just organizing into neat categories."

"Because of snow, mind ye talk now. It ain't yer fault the snow decided to come to pay a visit. Besides, I need to tell them we'll be having an extra setting at the New Year's table this year."

Lydia moved closer to Mark. "He asked."

"To go to his parents? That was fast."

"No, I've already met his parents. He asked me to marry him. Last night."

"I don't have a ring for her yet, but that's a technicality I plan to rectify as soon as we get out of here."

"Mark? Seriously?" Mary wanted to laugh and cry with happiness. "I love you guys. You know I prayed for this. I prayed I'd somehow be the one to bring the two of you together and was planning on playing matchmaker here at the resort. I didn't have to do a single thing."

Mark frowned. "Yes, ye did, Mary. Ye were the wee one that brought us together. Without ye, I wouldn't have met this jet-setting, high profile agent. I've got ye and yer dad to thank for that."

Mary brushed back tears. "Mark, you are the best thing. Lydia, I swear, this guy is a complete and ridiculous cornball of goofy love. Don't let the jokes fool you, he's an amazing man."

"I know. I've known for a while. I was just waiting for him to come around."

"How long has this been going on?"

Mark shrugged. "She's loved me a long time. I guess I had to move myself out of the way to see it."

Presley said, "Congratulations."

Mary stepped away. "Oh, you're still here."

He sighed. "I don't think I'm going anywhere, Mary."

"I don't want your songs anymore."

All three said at once, "What?"

"Can I just say this, please?"

"Mary, if you want me to tell you I don't have feelings for you, then I can't. If I have to lose this to be with you, I'll lose my writing for you. If it's about …"

"No, it's not about your feelings for me. It's not that. There's something else. I can't do this anymore, Mark."

"Do what?"

"This."

"Sit on a couch and drink coffee? Stand up, then. Turn to lemon water."

"This."

Mark looked to Lydia. "I'm confused. Am I missing something?"

Presley sat down beside her. "She doesn't want to sing anymore."

"I want to sing. Just not your songs. Not this way."

Lydia and Mark claimed the love seat beside her and leaned in. Lydia said, "He's winning awards with his songs. They're perfect for you. Every single hit was from him, Mary. You don't know what you're saying."

"I don't want to sing about clothes and shopping and breakups and heartaches, or suggestive lyrics that could be taken in a way that could lead someone to the wild side. My songs are a little wild now that I'm older, more about partying than I'd like."

Mark huffed. "You've lived a wild lifestyle, Mary. You fit the last songs."

"But what if I don't want to fit the songs? What if I want new songs that fit who I am?"

She found the words flowed so easily from her, even though she still questioned who she was.

Presley said, "I get it. I think I understand."

"You don't know me. What do you think you understand?"

Lydia said, "She must've seen the clip already. I knew you'd be angry, but I didn't think it'd drive you this far."

"What clip? What's happened now?"

Mark shook his head. "Never mind that. Go back to what ye were saying."

"She needs to know, Mark. You can't hide it from her. It'll be on every major broadcast station, and they'll probably even play it for the big game coming up next month."

"What are you talking about? Let me see it. Lydia, tell me what's going on?"

Lydia bit her lip. "You aren't going to like it, Mary. But I've already made some calls. Mark and I are going to get to the bottom of…"

"What is it, already? Show me."

Mary pulled out her phone and searched her name. She could find it herself. Nothing was showing except her last outburst in the National Observer Entertainment Heat about her attacking the press at the airport with some quotes she didn't remember saying in her anger. They loved to stretch the truth. Wait until they found out about her plans.

Mark's face was red when he spoke through clenched teeth, "It's hard to imagine the damage one person can do."

She looked at him and knew it was serious. That's why they were all coming down together. That's why they were wearing serious faces at first, and then had the awkward shifts, that turned to engagement talk as a deflection of easing into something big.

"Me? What did I do, Mark?"

"You signed it, Mary? How could you have done that? I thought I knew you. The principle behind the thing…"

"What thing? What did I sign?"

Presley held out his phone. "You might as well see it. But Mark, I'm telling you, she doesn't know. She wouldn't have done it."

Mary watched clips of her on stage, even one with her and Josey Wales together holding mics for the duet with a song dubbed over it, one she'd never sing, from some atrocious singer sounding like a tom cat scuffling. The lyrics were about getting drunk with her girls, and Josey's mouth was spouting it out along with her in some lip-synced craziness.

A photoshopped beer bottle was sitting on the amp beside Josey's wheelchair. Her signing autographs for fans while the company's logo was on the screen behind her. Yep, the zebra and the giraffe made an appearance. A circus show, and she was in the middle of it, smiling as if it were the most natural thing in the world. All edited in. All fake. All promoting the very thing her dad asked her to stay away from.

"I didn't sign that contract. I swear. It was Riff. I'm going to sue him for all he's worth. Get my money back what I paid him and then some."

Presley grabbed her hand, and she didn't snatch it away. "I knew you didn't sell out, Mary."

"Young girls follow me, Mark. It hurts me to think you'd even considered I'd do that. I'd never endorse the things he kept pushing my way. The shut-up conversation was the last straw, but his tirades had been building for months when I refused to falter at his ridiculous demands. Lydia, do something about it. The hair commercial was one thing. That's fine. The eye makeup. Fine. Not alcohol. They'll think I think it's cool to drink, and a young girl might go out and try it for the first time. Parents won't go for this. Josey's parents… What happens if they have a teen party and listen to my songs or see that commercial and do these things underage? What if they drive…"

Her voice caught and she pushed back the tears. The what ifs would submerge her into the depths of the ocean. "Please, Mark. Do something."

"Hire me as your manager and in the same week, I have to face the biggest fire of your career."

Mary said, "That's why you're now getting the big bucks. Just make it go away. Threaten to sue them. Anything. They have to pull these commercials today. He did it for spite. For being fired. He knew how I felt about this."

Lydia said, "I'll make it where he never works in this town again." She patted Mary on the leg. "I've always wanted to say that line. I heard it once from a movie. Trust me, no one will work with him if they think he'd ruin their career."

"All of this happened the minute I turned twenty-one. It wasn't just the beer commercial. The meetings and pitches kept coming for all kinds of 'new opportunities,' as he called them, for me to take the endorsements to the next millions, since I could be picked up with adult-themed content. Some of the things he actually asked me to do were over-the-top bad, ones I won't even discuss. I refused them all."

Presley said, "He even contacted me about songs for her for the new album. Songs her fans didn't need to hear. I told Mary I was uncomfortable with some of the songs I wrote for her, and already pulled the darkest one off the track. Never to see the light of day."

Lydia said, "And he was doing all of this behind our backs to make a buck. He's such a slime ball. I'm sorry I didn't see it happening, Mary." Then she turned her attention to Presley. "You should've contacted me."

"It didn't sit right with me. The news was giving her so much heat, and I feared she was changing."

"I was changing. I have changed. I'm a mess. We'll talk about that later. Right now, let's get this commercial removed from everywhere. Every place. Right now. Mark, I mean today."

"I know. Today. Let me start making calls." He kissed Lydia on the cheek. "I've got to handle this."

"I'm in it with you, dear. Let's go back to my room. Mary, don't you worry about a thing. Rest. Relax. Get your mind off of it. Mark will take care of it. I'll see to it."

He saluted. "Now I've got two women pressuring me to get the job done. I've got to keep my women happy."

"How am I supposed to not worry? How many people have already seen it? We can't know that. We can't know the damage it might've already done. I'll make a statement. Call the press. Let them know I'm here."

Mark pointed outside. "Even if they knew you were here, they can't get here. The roads, remember?"

"Then, I'll post a video on Instagram. That's all it'll take. My fans will spread it. I need to contact Josey and her family. I can't believe they involved her in this, all to hurt me, I know. Do you have her number?"

Lydia frowned. Worry was clearly spread across the lines of her face, even though she was telling Mary not to. "No. We worked through Make-A-Dream. Maybe they'll release it to me."

Presley said, "You have her email. Contact her that way."

Mary grabbed her phone and began forming the email as fast as she could. To hopefully make Josey laugh and not hate her, she attached the photo of the dog and sent it before Mark and Lydia could even make it up the stairs.

"That was fast. What did you say?"

"That it was all a misunderstanding and fake. An edited piece of junk, and not to let it bother her one bit. We'd take care of it or I'd be the outlaw between us."

"I'm sorry, Mary."

"Me, too." She hid her face in her hands. "My daddy would…" her voice broke with the hurt of it all.

"He would be spit-fire mad right now and probably threaten to punch that Riff guy."

"It's all my fault. I allowed this to happen."

"Wait. You signed the papers? I thought you said you didn't."

"I knew the pressure was on. It's been boiling over for months, and I didn't act as forceful as I should've. As soon as he asked me to do the ad, I should've torn the paper to shreds in his face and given him a warning. Then, the next ad opportunity doubled the money with the stipulation I'd have revealing parts in a movie. That's when I definitely should've said his contract was up. He can't come back on me and get me for a breach of contract because my dad made sure we had an open contract where I had authority to let him go without repercussions. He set me up just in case, and I'm so glad about that."

"I don't think jumping on social media solves anything. Hold off. Don't blast out a video yet. Let Mark and Lydia do their thing first, then you can say how you followed up with it."

"That requires patience. Something I don't have a lot of."

"Then, let's pray about that. I know you do pray, Mary."

Mary looked at him. Romantic. Bible quoter. Writer of love letters. A man who prayed. She moved from him then and leaned against the windowpane, imagining herself falling through glass, collecting shards.

"Don't run away from me, Mary," he whispered. He'd made his way to stand beside her. "I won't hurt you."

"Do you have a verse for being patient that doesn't involve love? I remember the one about love is patient..."

She didn't want to tell him that she'd looked up the verse he'd spoken to her and highlighted it in purple in her Bible app.

"I do."

"Well..."

"I thought you weren't talking to me."

"So, we're back to that. Do you want an apology for the way I've been treating you? Everyone?"

He reached for her hand and laced his fingers through hers. "That's close enough. Accepted. I've got one. I think it fits us right now. 'Rejoice in hope, be patient in tribulation, be constant in prayer.'"

"What's the hope? Hope that the video is removed before millions see it? How did you see it?"

"He sent the link to Mark, trying to be all funny."

"Then, I'll hope for deleting that junk for a start."

"I'm hoping for more than just a canceled ad."

"I'm hoping you'll know I can't be with you."

"I wrote you another song. One to replace the deleted track. Do you want to hear it?"

"Not really."

"Yes, you do," he chided as he nudged the side of her Converses. "It's about God."

"You wrote a song about God? You write Christian lyrics?"

"Mary, I'm a Christian. All of my lyrics have Biblical references in them somewhere. You didn't notice that?"

"No! I thought they were more about love and hurt and..."

"And life. My songs are about life. I should've given you the letters, but I didn't have the nerve."

"You had some nerve last night."

"It was that music, I'm telling you. I was hypnotized by the voice of Etta James."

"So, it had nothing to do with me at all?"

"Nope. Etta James, baby. She gets all the credit." He winked at her, trying the Mark charm advice. "Well, maybe you get a little bit of credit. Just a smidgen."

"A smidgen? I'll show you a smidgen."

She thought back on their dance and looked down at their hands, still entwined. Her heart hadn't calmed down from the race it was in, and she felt like she was doing laps. Calories were probably burning while she stood still.

He whispered, "Let's play name that line, and see if you can guess the reference. Are you ready?"

"You want to play a game, and I want to rear naked choke Riff."

"You're using fight terms now?"

"My dad and Mark were huge fans. I got them tickets to a cage fight before my dad got sick. They took me along, and the rest is history. I'm wondering if I could get a promoter to put Riff in the octagon."

"I'm trying to get your mind off Riff. He isn't worth your energy. The Lord will get him. Vengeance is mine, said the Lord. You know the truth. It doesn't matter what anyone else thinks."

"But it does matter. Especially after I wanted something more."

"Then, turn it all over to the Lord. Trust that Mark and Lydia can make things right. Trust that God can clear it. I'm praying for that now. Let's pray together, Mary. I'll start."

He bowed his head and began to pray without waiting on her to respond or stop him.

"Dear Lord, let the plans Riff has made to hurt Mary disappear. Let all threats against her cease. Let every ill thought, negative action, and hurtful thing be removed. Let the contract be severed and the video erased. Encamp angels around Mary. Soften Riff's heart, God. Teach him the error of his ways. Amen."

"Wait, did you just pray for Riff?"

"I did."

"And why would you do that? You were supposed to be praying for me."

"I think he needs more prayer than you do, Mary."

"I don't think so."

"I do. Would you ever spitefully hurt someone?"

"No, of course not!"

"Would you ever alter pictures or videos to include a child and play on the fact that she's dying of cancer?"

Mary pulled away at the thought. It sickened her. "Never. Oh, poor Josey."

"So, when I say that man needs more prayer than you right now, he does. The Lord can change Riff."

"Merv."

"Huh?"

"His name is Merv."

"Well, the Lord can change Merv," he said as he stifled a laugh. "As much as he needs to change his name. I knew Riff had to be fake."

"Like everything else about him."

"You aren't fake, Mary. Your fans know you. You're not perfect, but you aren't that video. You're just a girl in elf socks, with Stitch pajamas and a worn pair of Converses, innocent and sweet."

"You're only talking about my appearance, Presley. You don't know what I go through. How I battle against the tide."

"Then, let me know."

"Some things I can't put into words."

"That's why I write songs."

"But they're words, too."

"I can say they're inspired words, but it might be really what I'm feeling. Who would ever know except me?"

"The girl you write them for."

"Oh, yeah. Her. I'm talking to her now, and she's listening."

"Prayer works."

"It does."

"You're something else, Presley."

"That's what I've been told."

"By women?"

"One woman."

Mary knew it. She began to pull her hand away. Romantic. Bible quoter. Writer of love letters. A man who prayed. Cheater.

"No, Mary. Not that. My mom. I'm not in a relationship, if that's what's got you all worked up and inching away."

Mary glanced up at him, his eyes a darker blue now, resting close between sky and sea. "I'm scared of you," she whispered.

"You scare me, too. But being scared is a good thing."

"Not for me."

"Scared of losing something means it matters."

That was all she wanted. A life that mattered, and in her heart, she had the sneaking suspicion it would be more than she'd ever dreamed if she could only figure out how to let go and live in the moment with him.

Before Me

Presley's face took on a new meaning of gorgeous when he came back to her, excited to tell her the news. "They have one. It's in one of their conference halls."

"You get this excited when you know a piano is in the building?"

"I do. Come on," he said, as he grabbed her hand and practically pulled her down the hallway.

Mary took three strides to his one to play catch-up. When they entered the room, it was more than a place to hold a business meeting, she felt like she'd stepped into a 1940s jazz club. There was a stage with orchestra seating, and winged flared wooden cutouts crossing the pit in intricate designs. Chandeliers dropped low, and she imagined the glow of the room, with the dancers all doing the Charleston, a dance her grandmother once taught her in the living room while she wore her apron.

Mary felt like she was standing in a ballroom of memories. "Wow, this room is amazing."

"I bet the acoustics in here are great." He led her to the piano positioned on the side of the stage and opened the lid, sliding his fingers down the keys to check the tuning. "Perfect. It had to be, for me to share this with you."

"And what are we sharing again?"

"The song I wrote for you."

"You've written about fifty songs for me."

"Now that you put it that way, I'm mighty impressed with myself." He slid his glasses on and put his phone in front of him. "I might get nervous with you right here, so I need to see this."

"Which one are you going to play? Your new greatest hit?"

"The next greatest hit."

"And when did you write it?"

"Last night when you dumped me."

"I didn't dump you."

"Well, returning a love letter to someone pretty much sums up a dumping if I ever heard one."

"You have to be in a relationship to officially break up. You can't just end something that hasn't started yet."

"Well, technically, you almost did."

She stared at him, leaning against the piano and finding the words that could matter to him. "I'm glad I didn't. Bear with me, okay. I'll try."

"I'll take that."

"That's all I can say."

"I said I'll take that. I mean it."

He leaned over and gave her a hug, which she wasn't expecting at all. Maybe the first kiss, but not a hug. He was a hugger and an amazing one at that. She found her head nestled against his orange-and-blue flannel shirt and she could feel his pulse in his neck, pounding fast. He smelled so good that she closed her eyes, content to just stay there a while. She hadn't been hugged in so long, she'd forgotten how good it could feel. Maybe he was just good at everything.

A romantic, Bible-quoting, love-letter-writing, praying man who liked to hug. She sighed against him. "I could get used to this."

"Hugging strangers or hugging me?"

"You. Just you."

"If I don't sing to you now, I'm going to lose my nerve." He coughed and pushed himself away from her, and she could tell it was the last thing he wanted to do. "I've never sung in front of anybody before, except my family."

"And I bet they loved it."

"They claim to."

"You don't believe them?"

"No. I have such a strong accent, it's hard for me to drop it when I sing."

"Then, don't drop it. Own it. Let it be unique to you, and let that make you real."

"Your tone is like that, too. It's got this depth to it, a richness that is a mix between Southern rock and old rhythm and blues. It's like gold to a prospector. Me being the prospector, of course."

"Gold records come because of good songs. Anybody can sing. It's the lyrics that make them all."

"I disagree with you. Without the singer, we'd have words dead on a page. You bring my work to life."

"And you make me want to sing them. Your words are beautiful. I always imagined you an elderly man, gray-haired, filled with a happy life and so many experiences. You made me feel important when I sang your earlier songs, before Riff got a hold of you."

"Momma always said I was too serious and old before my time. For my eighteenth birthday, my brother mixed the candles around and put eighty-one instead, and they gave me an all-black, over the hill party. Between me and my brothers, I can rest assured say I'm the most mature one out of the lot. And I have lived a happy life, you've got that right."

"Go ahead, don't get me thinking about my past. Sing the present back to me, and make me forget with the melody."

"Sometimes melodies make you remember. That's the beauty of a new song. You never know which way it'll go until you get there."

"And did this one go as planned?"

"Not really. I was going to try to make a fast breakup song to get you to at least smile. A fun, upbeat one. Then, it took a dive to priorities."

"Oh, it's about that? Since I need to get mine straight."

"Don't we all."

"Just sing. No need to lecture."

"Okay. Don't judge my voice, now. Listen to the words."

Presley positioned his long fingers, and Mary watched as they moved fluidly across the lake of keys, like swans gliding. She felt more beside him when the music started than by the fireplace, in his arms, or against the softness of his neck.

And he wrote this song for her. Not Mary Bella but Mary Oxendine.

There was a deep, emotional quality to the way the notes rose and fell, lapping against the rowboat in her mind that she lounged on with him.

His voice wasn't bad. In fact, it was actually solid. It was country, with a twang that reminded her of the old classic singers when 8-tracks were popular, and it took her back to the moment her dad found a cardboard liquor store box at a yard sale once filled with them, and they had played them for hours since the paper had been pulled off many of them to reveal the secrets of the music behind the tiny black boxes.

Love God before me
That's the only way that we could ever be
Let's put God in the center
He'll take the helm and I'll enter
Into his gates with thanksgiving for me finding you
There's nothing we can't do
That a prayer between us can't move
I'm believing with all the faith I've got
That we can have a go at this life
And we can start when you're ready to
But you've got to love God before me
Baby, will you love God before me?

"I don't know what to say."

"You don't have to say anything."

"But I need to."

"Why? So many people think they have to fill the space with words."

"I'm like that."

"We can just sit here and play a little longer. Or we can sing it if you like. If you want to. You can sing it with me."

She wondered if she could find her voice in all the emotion settled right at the base of her throat.

"With you saying it like three times, I guess that means you want to sing it with me?"

"Maybe."

"I told you I'll try."

He started the song over, and Mary knew this was one she could play on repeat, the rest of her life, and never tire of hearing it.

"That's the way I imagined it. With your voice taking lead."

"I tried."

"You did. And you are trying. The way you're looking at me right now lets me know you are. The way you're sitting close to me lets me know you're trying really hard. How about if you don't have to try anymore. How about just be."

"Can you play that one? *Let It Be?*"

"Does everything I say remind you of a song?"

"That's actually not a bad thing. That means my heart listens to you, and it's speaking back in the language it knows best."

"Then I'll play whatever it is you want me to. All you have to do is ask, Mary."

"I did already. *Let It Be?*"

There was no room left for talking. The music spoke for itself. Mary's voice felt stronger than it ever had, and her heart was in the spaces between and all around them.

God, help me let it be, she thought as he played the notes. Let it settle into the hands of the romantic, Bible-quoting, love-letter-writing, praying man who gives the best hugs and who wants me to love You before him.

Wait and See

A few people trickled in and gathered around when they heard the music, and before long, there was a ballroom filled with patrons who were seated at the circular dining room tables enjoying the hotel entertainment, thinking it must be part of their package.

Mary didn't mind. She was on top of the world, and even sang the song from the Carpenters that her grandmother, Dessie, passed along to her as a song to be hers since her birth. Her grandmother played the guitar on the side porch, overlooking her collard plants, and mainly strummed church hymns while the clothesline sheets clapped along. She knew she got her love of music from her, because her daddy couldn't hold a tune to save his life.

"No one's recording it. No one knows it's you, probably. They're getting a free concert instead of paying a hundred bucks a seat."

"Well, it's good that their phones are away. It means they're enjoying themselves in the moment. Ask anyone if they would they like to pick a song. Let's see if we know it."

Presley asked the crowd for any requests and someone called out, "*Mary, Did you Know*," which happened to be one of Mary's favorite Christmas songs.

It wasn't just because she was named after Mary, but it was the simple, yet powerful imagery the song evoked in her mind. She felt like she could witness the scene of

Mary holding her baby, questioning and marveling in all that God had done.

After she sang it, the whole room erupted in thunderous applause. Mark and Lydia walked in and came to stand by them, waving at them to get their attention. They had news. She could tell.

They left the room and the patrons behind. Presley said, "That's what you need. That kind of music. That was powerful, Mary."

"I need a Christmas album?"

Lydia said, "That's not a bad idea. And the good news is you don't need a lawyer, not yet anyway. That's a positive sign. Now, let's get some lunch."

Presley took Mary's hand and led her to the small café. They got a corner booth away from the bar crowd, and all settled in. As soon as they ordered burgers and fries, the talk turned to business again. Mary was relieved that there didn't have to be any litigation involved.

Mark said, "All of that for nothing. That scoundrel. He dubbed that and edited it himself, probably on some free app. He only sent it to me in a link. There was no contract with the company. They had no knowledge of the video existing. He just did it as a warning. Said he was coming for us. Let him try."

"He has nothing on me," said Mary. "We can get a lawyer. That sounds like a threat to me."

"We've turned it in to your attorney for the files. Mark forwarded the original email, made calls to the marketing team to stop any contact with Riff, and let all of the companies you're contracted with know that you have a new manager and to have no discussions or dealings with ol' Merv. The scare is over, Mary. There's nothing to worry about."

Mark passed her a sticky note. "Here's Josey's number. The Make-A-Dream Foundation advocate was thrilled ye wanted to reach back out to Josey."

Mary had forgotten to check her emails. There was no message from her. "I'll call her now."

Mary let the phone ring until Mrs. Wales' voice message picked up. Mary left her number and prayed they'd call back so she'd get a chance to reassure the family nothing was happening with the video.

She turned to Presley and said, "Thanks for calming me down earlier and not letting me make some public statement. That would've been so ridiculous, with me acting all frantic and freaking out, for nothing."

"People would've suspected you might be losing your edge, apologizing for something you hadn't done." He winked at her, and she smiled back.

"And thank you for standing by me, and the singing…the song…my soul needed that."

"Music has that way. That's how they fought battles in the Old Testament."

"With music?"

"Before armies. Worship was a type of warfare. It also brought peace to a madman like Saul. Music changes people."

"And you know all this about the Bible because?"

"My daddy is a gun-toting preacher. Remember when I told you he had a shooting range and was an instructor, well, he also instructs people in the ways of the Lord."

"He has his own list of traits, huh?" Mary wondered if someone made a list about her, what would they come up with? Probably some that she'd be ashamed of.

"What do you mean?"

"Never mind."

"And so, they're talking," chuckled Mark. "Once you get Mary going it's hard to get that girl to stop."

"Alright now, Mark. If we're going to start that, I've got some things I could share with Lydia that just might …"

"Make her fall in love with me even more. I'm a gem, baby."

"A slim Jim."

"There is nothing slim about my muscles. See." Mark flexed, and he did still have it for an older man. She'd give him that.

Lydia said, "Mary, I think you need therapy."

"What?

Mark said, "Well, that came out of the blue. There could've been a better time to address this."

Presley put down the cup he was holding and some of the water sloshed on the table. "I think that's not the right way to say it, either."

"What is the right way? Mary, you've been struggling for years, honey. I want you to see someone."

Mary couldn't believe what she was hearing. "I have therapy. Music therapy. It's all I need. I'm writing, too. I've been writing some songs of my own." She thought about the song she wrote, *GPS*, she needed some God Pointing Steps right now. Away from the table and eyes of pity. Anything but that.

Mark squeezed her hand. "That's good, Mary. But we're talking about yer dad, God bless his soul. He wouldn't want you to be so miserable, honey. And not to mention yer mom and what she's done. There's anger in ye that ye got to deal with or it will always deal with ye."

"I've made up my mind about something, Mark. It's why I really wanted both of you here. Having Presley here makes perfect sense to me now. It's letting me see I have at least one person that will be willing to go with me to the other side."

"The other side? Don't start talking scary stuff, Mary. If you've been considering…"

"No!" Mary said, a little too loud, "The other side of the business. I'm over this life, this way, Mark. I can't do it anymore. I can't be around the Riffs of the world. I need to tell you something."

Mark leaned over, his eyes intent on Mary, and she could tell he was probably fearing for his own position with her in the business. Everything depended so much on her decisions, and she'd done so poor a job at it. It was time to change.

Today.

Now.

"I want to be a Christian artist. I want to speak about Jesus. I can't do that right now. The industry has me so scared to breathe. I wasn't able to share my heart for the Lord, like He was a loser, and I was the one that was losing out. All these years, I've had to hide it. When Daddy died, a part of me gave up. I threw away my Bible. I was over it all but Jesus came in and showed me the truth. Daddy wasn't gone, just a blink to eternity with Him, and one day, when it was my time, I'd get there, too. I want to write songs about hope, and patience, and belief." She paused to smile at Presley. "I want to write about love and encourage young girls to know they're not alone. It might feel like it sometimes, but they aren't. I'm not. I want to stop denying Jesus, Mark. Please, let me do this."

Lydia leaned back in the booth and slipped her hand through Mark's arm. "I don't know much about the worship industry, Mary."

Mark said, "Your Daddy sure would be proud of you. He'd say it's about time you started making decisions for yourself around here and he'd follow you to the moon and back or a church pew or the GMA awards show, because you could get there, you know."

Presley said, "I'm here for the long haul. I'm not planning on going anywhere but where you are."

Lydia said, "I'm with him. You still want me on your team, even though I'm not in it with the language of gospel music? It's something I'll do for you, Mary, because I love you like a little sister. And I love this manager of yours, that is if you still want him, too. I promise I'll try."

Presley squeezed Mary's hand. "Trying is where it starts."

"None of you are going anywhere. Ever since I sang with Josey Wales, I knew I wanted to cross over. Something happened to me, my spirit opened up. She's been praying for me. I wonder if it was for this? Anyway,

I was so nervous to tell you, that you'd think I wasn't serious or you'd try to talk me out of it."

"I've been so scared for ye, Mary. I've been watching ye falter for years, and all I've wanted was to see ye get on track. This could be exactly the change ye need to make a difference. We need to thank that little girl, proper. When we get out of here, let's go and visit her. Take her a keyboard and some musical instruments. Let that singer have her own studio and a place to write her music."

"Mark, that's the best idea! I love it!"

Presley said, "Can I come along, too? I'd like to meet another songwriter. I haven't met another one, other than you, Mary. Speaking of. I'd love to see some of your lyrics."

"They're no comparison to what you can do."

"It isn't a contest."

"True. I'll show you one day. When I trust you enough not to go plagiarizing my stuff." She laughed and turned to Lydia. "I have my newest song I want to sing. Presley wrote it for me last night."

Mark said, "Last night? That was fast."

Lydia asked, "What's the name of it?"

"*God Before Me.*"

"You knew about her wanting to go to Christian music?"

"No, I'm a Christian. I love worship music, so I tend to mix traditional in with the contemporary feel. I wrote the song to her to let her know that if we keep God first and center, we'll make it through whatever."

"And that means a new career path, unknown territory, a past that's bound to catch up with me, and a momma on the run."

Mark said, "What about all the plans for having you do movies? I know that was on the horizon."

"Not the kind of movies Riff was setting up. They were movies with inappropriate scenes, Mark. He saw me as an adult and wanted to put me in every situation possible, regardless of how I kept saying I wouldn't compromise. He must've thought if he'd kept pressuring me, I'd break. I was close a couple of times, especially when I was going through that patch with Momma and then Darian, and thought of ways I could get back at them, but I'm so thankful I somehow always got the strength to say no. I want to get away from that life. I don't want Hollywood anymore. I just want Jesus."

Lydia piped up, "Maybe the South suits us, Mark. You want to go ahead and find us that retirement home pre-retirement? Let's go across the county and live in the extremes. No middle ground. We're either left or right, and I'd rather be on the right side."

Mary said, "I need a slower pace. I need a home base that's away from all the lights, where I can actually see the stars without the smog."

"I could put a call in to my daddy. He could help."

"If you tell me he's a gun-instructor preacher who sells real estate, I think it's going to be hard to look at him with a straight face."

"What?" Presley laughed. "No. He knows a lot of farmers and can help you see about fair prices."

Mark said, "I'll take ye up on that offer. We can work on that later today. Right now, I want to take care of this burger in front of me. I told ye once Mary gets you to talking, the world stops."

"The world stopped the minute I knew that girl was mine."

"Don't let it stop, Presley. Let it keep going. Let it keep spinning. I don't want to stop your world, just be beside you in it."

No Way

Jasper interrupted Mark's plans of dessert. "It's best we move along now."

Mark stood up immediately, his joking face aside. "What is it?"

"There's been another call in to the owners from the caretaker that lives on the corner lot of the property. His house was broken into."

Mary's hairs on the back of her neck stood up in response to Jasper's announcement. "The sleigh robbery and now a home? We're safe here, right, Jasper?"

"I'm here," he said, and his steely voice provided comfort.

Presley said, "We're snowed in here, anyway. It's not like we can go anywhere."

"Neither can the criminal. If whoever it is comes this way, they don't know what they're stepping into. We've already updated the resort security. They're aware of our training."

Mary's phone rang.

Jasper grabbed it from her before she could answer it. "Allow me, ma'am." He tried to smile but his face still held the stoic lines of chiseled rock. "Hello. Yes, she's here. Thank you and hold on. It's Mrs. Wales."

Mary stood up and took her phone back. "Thanks, Jasper, for always looking out for me."

She moved to the side and out of the way of the servers, but she could still feel their eyes on her. They must've thought this was about her. Somehow it probably was.

"Mrs. Wales, how is Josey?"

"She's fine, dear. She's hanging in there."

"If you got a chance to see the email, it was all a hoax about the video. There's nothing to worry about. My lawyers are on standby if there is."

"What email?"

"The one I replied back to Josey."

"Oh, no, honey. Josey hasn't emailed you. I'm so glad you found a way to contact us. We lost your email address the night of the concert. In all of the rush to get off the stage, it somehow made its way out of Josey's bag."

"No way."

"Yeah, we're so sorry about that. Josey has been so upset that she didn't have a way to contact you."

"Now that you have my number, text me her real email, and I'll send her a new one."

"She's down the hall getting some tests run now. She'll be so sad she didn't get a chance to hear from you."

Mary got the information for the hospital and told her of their surprise plans of bringing music to Josey as soon as they were out of the storm. Mrs. Wales cried over the phone but before hanging up, she said they'd been praying for her every night.

"Are you sure Josey didn't send me the email?"

"No, dear. I'm sure. We've been here at the hospital for an extended stay since the concert."

"Let me ask you this, does Josey pray the same thing about me every night but doesn't know why?"

"Yes, but how would you know that?"

"I don't know what's going on, Mrs. Wales, but give me a little time, and I'll call you back."

"Please do. Josey will love that."

"I promise. Bye."

They hung up and she handed her phone back to Jasper.

"Mary, I heard parts of that. Someone has your IP address."

"I emailed someone that I thought was Josey."

Jasper frowned. "Give me the entire conversation, please. Forward it."

"That's not all. If it wasn't Josey, then someone knows their whereabouts, too. I'm more concerned for her family than I am for me. Jasper, can you somehow cover them?"

Lydia said, "Why would whoever this is involve Josey and her family?"

"To get to me. The email had too much information. A conversation, even. A prayer. Please, Mark. We've got to make sure they're okay."

Mark said, "I've got some old military contractor buddies in Tennessee. Is she still at St. Jude Children's Research Hospital?"

"Yes."

"Then I'll take care of that immediately. I'll call Mr. and Mrs. Wales. There'll be someone with them within the hour."

Presley said, his voice low and shaky, "The world has gone to hell in a handbasket."

"Eighty-one-year-old comment, there, guy," she sighed heavily. "We've got Jasper and the team. I'm not concerned."

Jasper said, "I guarantee they went to the caretaker house first, thinking Mary would've rented her own cabin. They're here." He spoke code into his hidden mic. "Move."

"So, where are we headed, exactly?"

"To my room."

"Jasper. We don't need to hold up in one room."

"We need to do exactly what Jasper says," said Mark.

"I can't believe this is happening. It's Christmas Eve, isn't it?"

Lydia said, "Yes, it is. We had reservations tonight in the ballroom for a holiday show."

Jasper replied, "We can get room service just fine."

"All day? All of us?"

"Until the morning, Mary. The break in the storm will be overnight, and I'll have a helicopter come to take us out of here if I have to arrange it. We'll stop by and get whatever you need from your room."

She thought of being stuck all day and night with all of them together in one room and having a chilling tales slumber party with a creeper stalking her. It wasn't her idea of a Christmas party.

Lydia said, "I think we should take all our things with us into one location. Clear it out. Make it look like we all left, just in case. They probably wouldn't consider Jasper and your security team. They'll be looking for you."

"That's an idea I like," said Jasper. "Get everything."

Mark said, "How big is your room?"

Mary answered, "I know you're referring to my luggage. I pack light."

"Sure, Mary. Just wait and see, Presley. Ye can be the judge."

"Oh, I'm not going to get in the middle of a conversation about a woman and her luggage."

"Good point. You see I haven't spoken a word to Lydia about her smashing idea."

It took them a few minutes to collect all of their things and the entire time, Mary had a detail with her, helping her pack up swiftly and without sound. This was part of her life now. No one else in the resort was aware there was a stalker around. No one probably even knew of the caretaker break-in.

Once, an obsessed fan had found her home and spray-painted her gate before being captured and charged. She was chased more than she could count by aggressive paparazzi who swarmed her like wasps, always ready to strike.

It was so unnerving, knowing someone could be in any of the rooms, waiting for them.

Waiting for her.

∞∞∞∞

Jasper's suite was connected by doors on both sides to two other rooms, which held her security team. Jasper talked about the quick construction it took to make the resort fit their needs.

"You mean, you built these doors before I came?"

"On the day you came. We wanted to make sure you didn't change your plans and ruin their property. The owners obliged, said it would work well for them for future family suites and wedding parties. Besides, they get to have your picture as a guest and plaster you all over their site once we walk out the back doors."

Lydia asked, "How can everyone be so calm?"

Mark gave her a quick hug. "We're here, honey. There's nothing that's going to happen."

"How can you guarantee…" She let her own sentence drop.

Mary knew there were no guarantees in life. Her father had finally sought out a counselor, taking medications for his depression and talking more to Mark about his PTSD, even finding ways to give back to wounded warriors on their trips across the country. One day her dad was calling her Miss Mary Mack, the next day he said, "Mary, I might not come back."

Presley sat down beside her on the couch. He had two bags between his feet. "This is me."

He unzipped his black bag, and it was filled with notebooks.

"Wait. Where's your clothes?"

"In the other one."

"And you carry all of these books with you?"

"Just in case."

"Of what? A fire? So you can bring your most precious treasures with you? Grab your bag and run?"

"Can I see?"

"My notes? Sure. If you trade."

Mary thought about her writing. She had a song right behind her heart. One she'd wanted to write for so long, but she felt she'd be taken out to sea and left to drown if she wrote it on paper. Much less sang it.

She found her head resting on his shoulder. She needed a moment.

"I like this." Mary eyed him sideways but put her head back down. "Not in these circumstances, but still. It's nice to have you right here with me."

"Will you help me?"

"Yes, of course, I will."

"Will you write a song for my…"

She couldn't even say it. She couldn't, because if she said it, all the ways about him that she loved would come back. They came back in waves anyway, but never a Tsunami.

"Your dad?"

"Hmm…mmm."

"Tell me about him."

"Remember When was close as you ever came. It was like you had a glimpse of us in the open field across from the railroad tracks where we once lived back in Robeson County, flying cheap kites in long plastic bags."

Mark said, "Buck was a hero. He won a Silver Star."

Lydia added, "He was always looking out for Mary. That was his baby girl. She was his heartbeat."

"And he was mine," she whispered.

Mark said, "He stepped into the role of a fierce protector as soon as she was born."

Jasper chimed in, "He drove an old 1955 Chevy and loved 49ers football. He was a golden rule man."

Mary got up and excused herself. The only place she could go to be alone was the bathroom. It wasn't long and Lydia was knocking.

"Are you okay?"

"I'm fine."

She knew she'd turned to Mark. "She's saying she's fine again."

Presley was there. "That means she's not fine. Can I come in?"

"In the bathroom?"

"No," he said in a joking tone. "Yes. Of course, where else?"

Mary wiped her face and pulled her scrunchie from her arm and tied her hair up. She opened the door and smiled. "I was just fixing my hair."

"You're fine?"

"Yes. Fine."

"Then, sit with me a while."

"Where? On the toilet? I don't think so."

"In the bathtub. Trust me."

"You want me to get into a bathtub."

"Stay here." He came back with pillows and one of the folded blankets from the hall closet and lined the bathtub. He took his boots off and stepped inside with his electric guitar socks on.

She followed him, even though she felt absolutely ridiculous, and found herself fitting better in the tub than he did.

Mark popped in and said, "What in the world?"

"I'm about to write a song. Care to join us?"

"No, thanks. I don't think there's room."

Mary asked, "Do you always write songs in the bathtub with your clothes on?"

"Sometimes I do. This is where I first started writing and wanted to share it with you. I was in third grade and my teacher had an old clawfoot tub in our classroom. If we were good, we'd get chances to sit in the bathtub and read or write."

"And you got your chance?"

"I was a very good boy, thank you very much. I always got to sit in there, and I wrote my first song. It was about the things I saw around me in the classroom, and it was from my view from the bathtub, peeking out. The fascination of it all. The thrill. I never want to lose that. So, sometimes I fix up the bathtub just like this and capture that feeling back."

Mary leaned back. She liked that story. "So, you think I'll feel safer here, writing words in a bathtub?"

"It is a little silly. Maybe it will free up your mind."

"Just give it time," she said. "Wait. I want that line in the song somewhere. Everyone told me I'd get over losing my dad. Give it time, they'd say. How much time do I need? I lose him over and over again, every day. It doesn't go away."

She climbed out of the tub.

"Wait. We're just getting started."

"I need my journal, too."

When Mary came back, she peeked over his arm. "You've already got a few lines. Can you share?"

He passed the book to her. "If you don't like it, I understand. It's pressure with you looking at me."

She said, "You can read my GPS song I wrote while I read this. Maybe you can doctor it up."

Mary held his journal in her hand and realized this was different than receiving an email, a digital image. She loved the loops and swirls of his handwriting, focusing on the surface things first and easing herself into the deep end.

Just give it time
That's the line I keep replaying
That's what everybody's saying
But that doesn't heal the wounds

Just give it time
There's no way around it

I'm faced with it on the daily
And I can't turn the clock back now

So, all I can do is
Pray and hope to hold on to
The good and lovely thoughts of you
Just give it time

Mary closed the book. "I love it. How did you write that fast? I don't understand where it comes from."

"I give all the credit to Jesus, Mary. It's not me. I'm not smart."

Jasper called out, "I think you're smart."

"Are we wired? Do you have mics in the bathroom?"

Mark said, "Mary, when you sing you don't need a mic. Besides, the door is open."

Presley said, "What did you think?"

Lydia called out, emotion in her voice, "Beautiful."

Presley leaned over and leaned his face against his knees. "You're beautiful."

She whispered, "I thought you said I was cute."

"You still are. But your soul is a beautiful thing. You're like an ornate box, carved with all these experiences that have scarred you, but when you open the latch, a delicate ballerina begins to spin to the slow wind of Swan Lake."

"My box usually has a key. I don't go handing it out to anyone."

"I know." He grabbed her hand and kissed her there, in the middle of her palm. "A star in the palm of your hand."

"Can we add more to the song now or is your bathtub inspiration gone?"

"No, baby. I'm ready. Give me back my book. And if I might say, I loved GPS. You could take that one on the road, for sure."

"Maybe."

"Now, let's go to the verses. You know the way it sounds now. How you just picked up my words and sang it like that, you talk about how I could write that fast. How did you know how it would go? We don't even have any instruments."

"I hear them playing in my head. Always piano, violins, and a cello. It's what's been happening every time I try to write one. When I saw your lyrics, they started up again in my head and played until we were done. They keep playing now, wanting an audience."

"Every artist has a process. I respect that."

"Like I respect the tub."

"I told you! This is where it happens! You should try it when I'm not around."

"Maybe not."

"I hope ye take baths, Mary."

"Mark, really. You're still out there listening?"

Mark answered, "Of course we are. Keep writing. Let us hear our little bird sing."

Mary and Presley went back and forth on the verses and developed the chorus more. The song was coming together and in less than thirty minutes of Daddy's Little Girl, she sang the bridge with tears streaming down her face.

I know you're waiting on the other side for me
You had your faith that's one thing I never had to
doubt
Along with your love for me
And all the times it's hurt me that you're gone
I know your heart still lives on
It's a place I keep
Tucked deep within me
I'll always be
Daddy's little girl

Writing was a little easier with Presley's hand in hers. She felt her father all around, and knew her heavenly Father was with her, too.

Lord, this song could help bring peace to someone, she thought. Let that peace begin with me.

Reach Out

Jasper's suite wasn't the most optimum to having Christmas Eve dinner, but they made due. It had a small wooden farm table with benches, enough to fit six people. Lydia put in a call to the owner, and an elaborate spread was delivered for everyone in the sleepover party, along with a Christmas centerpiece and tableware to create a festive atmosphere in the otherwise gray room.

Her security team shared their meals around the couch and chairs and left both doors open to move in and out of both adjacent rooms, having their own space, but still keeping surveillance.

As light as the conversation was among them, Mary couldn't help but worry about Josey.

Mark broke into her thoughts. "I've already got a team there, Mary. Come back to us."

"I'm here."

Lydia said, "Your heart is in Tennessee."

Mary turned to Presley with a smile. "Now, that sounds like another song we could write."

"Do you want to go back to the bathroom?"

"Maybe later," she said, turning back to her untouched food. "What if he hurts one of you."

"Who is he?"

"This stalker."

Jasper spoke from the couch. "He won't. I'm here."

"I keep hearing that from you, Jasper."

"It's true. We're trained for this. We aren't trained just to stand by and watch you enter and exit a building and step into a car at an airport."

"My mercenaries."

"At your service."

Lydia said, "Enough of that talk. Let's change the subject. Mary, can we talk more about your transition?"

"Have you scheduled the national tour yet?"

"No. I was waiting until the new year. Something told me to hold back on the dates. I see why. It all makes sense. Glad I still have ears to hear."

"And a heart to understand," said Lydia. "If you leave Mary Bella behind, you'll also lose a lot of supporters. The music you've built has really impacted the industry."

Presley said, "Don't gain the world and lose your soul. Better to be Mary Oxendine than to give yourself away."

Mary stood up and began to pace. "I'm thinking of still making a video."

Mark grabbed her hand. "You don't need to apologize for Riff's video mashup. It was a fake."

"No, a video talking to the fans. They can replay it after the shock wears off. They can hear it straight from me and not from some news reporter or a publicist."

Mark asked, "Saying what?"

"That I'm now following my heart to Christian music. It's what I can give myself for Christmas."

"You sure you don't need a sweater?" Mark replied. "It could get ugly really quick."

"Or it could get supportive. I'm going that way regardless of how it goes. I don't want to stop singing. It's what I do. It's all I know how to do. I just need to sing for Jesus, not for me."

Presley said, "Sing the song you wrote for your daddy."

"Now?"

"No. On the video."

"But we don't have a studio or the band."

"You've got your guitar."

"How about Before Me? That one is better."

"That one is for later. Don't let that song be the one they know you by. Let it be in honor of your father. That would matter more to you than anything. To associate the day you gave your career to Jesus and sang a song about your father."

Mark patted Presley on the back. "This is a smart one, I'm telling ye. He's a keeper."

Lydia said, "Your daddy sure knew what he was doing to have that contest."

"What contest?"

"The radio contest. He came to me with the idea. I'll never forget it. He said, 'There's a perfect song for Mary out there. A writer who'll do right by her. Let's have a nationwide contest.' That's how we found Presley."

Presley looked shocked. "That was your dad? The one that called me? I figured it was just someone you hired."

Mary held back tears. "What did he say?"

"He said he loved my song, and that he wanted to hire me straight on to be your full-time songwriter. I couldn't believe it. Just from Remember When. He said his favorite line was I remember when you saved me, and it all made perfect sense. He knew I was talking about Jesus. He told me to never do you wrong. That's why he had that fatherly tone. I promised him I wouldn't. I was hired. The next day, I met Lydia. I was eighteen years old, a freshman in college, now a songwriter for a famous girl who climbed the top 100 charts faster than anyone of her time. Singing my songs. And it all started with a contest and Remember When."

"Daddy actually went through the contest songs himself? He found Presley?"

"He did. He would stay up half the night going through them. He said, 'I don't know how this young boy gets it. That's the kind we need for Mary.'"

Mary sat back down beside Presley and looked at him. "So, we can thank my dad for us."

"I'll thank him every day for the rest of my life for seeing something in my words that made him choose me."

"It's more than the song," said Mark. "Buck had a way about him. Maybe it was intuition, a strong sense or heavenly intervention, but he could always tell about the integrity of a thing at just a glance."

Lydia said, "That's why he never liked Riff."

"What if it's Riff? What if he's here to hurt me?"

Mark bellowed, "He doesn't have the nerve. Ye saw how he hid behind the video. He's a coward, Mary. And don't forget the most important part of it that tells me it's not him: he knows about yer security team. He wouldn't dare come into this den of bears."

Presley said, "Let's focus on what we can control. Like making that video. I think it's a good idea."

"Now you like my plea to the fans."

"It's not a plea. You won't have to beg anyone to like you. Your fans love you."

"Apparently, one loves me too much."

Lydia said, "Stop spiraling about what's happening outside these doors. Presley's right. I think you need to do the video and honor Buck by playing the song you wrote for him. That's a way to start telling people. You've got that part in there about heaven and how life goes on with Jesus in eternity. You're singing to many people with that song, Mary. I don't know of anyone who hasn't lost somebody. Something. In some way."

"I don't know if I'm ready to sing it. We don't have the melody all down yet, and I didn't write it alone."

Presley said, "We co-authored it. I co-author all of my songs, so I'm used to it."

Lydia acted surprised. "This is the first I've heard tell of this. You've got a ghost writer?"

"No, the Holy Spirit writer. The author and finisher of our faith."

Mary said, "I think that means I need to practice."

Mark pushed her plate toward her. "Eat first, and then practice. This isn't the first threat we've had. You can't let it get to your nerves."

"Just because it isn't the first, doesn't mean it gets any easier. Why do people have to be so cruel? What do they want from me?"

Mark shook his head and sighed. "People can be twisted, Mary. In ways we can't even begin to understand."

The lights flickered and then cut off. Jasper used his cell light and commanded one of his men to go check the breaker.

A report from one of the men came in after a minute of silence. "It's just the storm. Nothing was tampered with."

"It's clear."

It was as if everyone released their breath all at once.

Lydia said, "How's that for a holiday show? I'm sure that's been canceled. Everyone will go back to their rooms anyway."

Jasper said, "That's actually safer. I'd rather have them tucked away than freely roaming while someone with foul intent could be under their noses."

Presley squeezed Mary's hand. "Play for us, Mary. We'll get some emergency candles and lights set up. The music will keep our minds off of all this."

Mary grabbed her guitar, sat on the carpet, and spread open the journal. They didn't play any chords while writing, and Mary still needed to figure out the tune. Presley didn't play the guitar, so he couldn't help her. He didn't have a piano tucked away in his bag.

She prayed for the Lord to help her through this. There was a mad person out there after her. A storm was raging outside. The devil was nipping at her heels.

Mary stopped strumming and looked up at Presley, who'd made his way down beside her. "What if I sing it all at once, and it breaks my heart."

He gave a light tug to one of her curls that had escaped her scrunchie. "I told you this before, and I'll say it again, there is beauty in a new song. Singing it for the first time. You never know which way it'll go until you get there."

"So, it could break my heart, or I could have a piece of my heart back, is that what you're getting at."

"Get there. You'll see. Either way, you're not alone, Mary. We're here."

"I know," she said.

And she did. She looked around the room. Lydia and Mark were busy unpacking boxes that one of the hotel staff assistants had brought in. They were lighting candles and stealing quick kisses in between the flickering of growing shadows on the walls. She imagined one as her daddy waving at her from a crowd, cheering her on.

The men were on screens and headset communications. Jasper gave her a thumbs up when her eyes fell on him. She turned to Presley and saw the way his eyes shone for her in the dark, and she scooted a little closer to him. She marveled in the calm strength he carried about him. There were no lines of concern on his face, only something she recognized clearly now with a guitar between them and a song at her feet.

He loved her.

His smile grew wider the more she stared at him, and she watched the outline of his cheeks grow a little redder when she didn't turn from him.

She loved him.

In all of the ways she'd never felt for another man. A tenderness took over her, and she knew this kind of love did hold God in the center of it. By finding God again, she found who she was.

She was no longer a girl lost in a haze, confused, or misguided.

The truth was she was loved. Loved by the people in this room. And he was right, they were there for her. She found comfort in knowing that God was there, too.

"I think it's time I sing the song, now," she whispered.

"What's been stopping you?"

She was almost breathless. "You."

"But I haven't said anything."

"Your heart's talking to me, and I stopped to listen."

"Did your heart speak back?"

"Yes."

"And what did it say?"

"It said I love you, too."

Presley's eyes danced, the candle glow dancing across his face. "Then that's enough for me."

I can't believe you're gone

None of this makes sense as my life carries on

I can't stop the sink hole from widening and I feel I'm falling

Fast

How long will this grief last

Will it ever go away or

will I be reminded every day of what I've lost

Just give it time

That's the line I keep replaying

That's what everybody's saying

But that doesn't heal the wounds I'm facing

Just give it time
There's no way around it
I'm dealing with it on the daily
And I can't turn the clock back now

So all I can do is
Pray and hope to hold on to
The good and lovely thoughts of you
Just give it time

First Take

Everyone clapped when she was done. The room had taken on a new feeling. It was hard to put a word to a powerful wave of emotion that hung on the last strum and emitted out. No amp needed. No stage. No lights other than the candles, almost at a standstill holding breaths in reverence, then taking on the slow dance after the fingers ceased to applaud.

"You have incredible timing," Lydia said. "It's so authentic what you do. That song will be your next hit."

"You say that like you know."

"I've never been wrong before. I'm waiting any day now for the phone to ring to tell us about our Song of the Year nomination. That shiny gramophone will look nice on your shelf. We've already got the tickets for you, Presley. You can take two people with you. We'll set you up in style."

"My parents, definitely. They'd love it. Nashville is a place they've always wanted to travel to. My daddy has a thing for the Grand Ol' Opry. Still watches YouTube clips of old Hee Haw shows."

As if on cue, Lydia's phone rang. "There's the winning call now. I knew it was coming." She glanced down in excitement, then her face did a three sixty dramatic turn for the worst.

Mark said, "What is it?"

"It's Madeline."

"Don't," Mary said. "Just don't. Don't even pick it up."

Presley asked, "Who's Madeline?"

"My mother."

Lydia said, "What if it's important? It could be about the case. We have plans next week to …"

Mark scowled. "Let it go to voicemail. When we get back to the real world, we'll deal with her."

Mary breathed a sigh of relief. She didn't even want to hear the voice of her mother through the speaker, and as loud as she talked, there would be no avoiding the tone.

"Thanks, Mark."

"No problem. Besides, we've got a video to make. Who's got some fancy equipment?"

Jasper held up his surveillance iPad. "It's got a good camera if you want me to record anything. Just don't go to the home screen. You might see some of my kids downloaded some apps on there. Ruby is learning her ABCs and there is this jet pack game that Mike loves to play."

Mary laughed. "I've seen you play that game, Jasper. It's okay. Old people can be gamers, too."

Jasper said, "It passes the time. Before we video, what are you going to say? Do you need to rehearse something?"

"No. I'm just going to say whatever comes to me."

Presley said, "I think we should pray first."

"Good idea." Mary had been whispering prayers to God all day.

Presley led the group in prayer. At the close, everyone gathered around Mary and gave her words of encouragement.

"You've got this, Mary."

"You'll do great."

"He's looking down on you."

"He'd be proud of who you've become."

"Stay strong, Mary."

"The Lord is with you."

She pulled her hair out of her scrunchie and smoothed it down. "How do I look? Do I need anything?"

Presley gave her a hug. "You're lovely."

"Cute. Beautiful. Lovely. I see I'm evolving."

"Possibly."

Mary's arms went around his waist and she leaned against him. He was warm.

"Mary. If you want to shoot this video, let's do it. We've all set up the room for you."

Mary stepped away from Presley in a daze. She glanced around and the room hadn't changed much. They added the throw pillows back on the couch and moved some of the candles to line the counter around her. The centerpiece was off to the side, adding a touch of red against the gray walls.

"Thanks, everybody. Thanks for doing all this."

Jasper said, "No problem. We'll set up the camera here and hit record when you're ready."

She cradled her guitar and looked at Presley. "Will you sit with me?"

"I'll just be over here, Mary. It's not like I can go anywhere. I think you should do this on your own. Not alone, but on your own. You know what I mean."

"You're right." She let out a heavy breath and closed her eyes. "I need the words, Lord," she whispered. "Give me the words."

She turned to the camera and nodded. It was time to speak her truth. Let it fall, Lord. Let it fall and be heard. Let her voice sound strong, even though she didn't feel strong. Let her words matter to someone. To anyone. To her daddy. To her. It was time it mattered.

Let Me Introduce You

Jasper gave her the sign. It was recording.

"Hey everybody, it's me, Mary. It's Christmas Eve, if you aren't catching this tonight, I want you to know when it all changed for me. Oh wow. I just got the significance of that. Funny how sometimes you're in the middle of a day and it all goes one way, you would've never planned it, but it's happening. On this very night, there's somebody I want to introduce you to. I'm in a relationship."

She looked over to Presley and saw the shock on his face. He held his hands up as if to protest but she kept speaking, looking back to the camera without calling him over.

"You might've heard of him. He's sacrificed a lot for me, everything, really. And I've let him down. I can't believe he never broke up with me. He never turned his back on me. Not once. Even when I was angry. Even when I couldn't think straight from fear. I have fears. Fears about my mom. Fears about life and what's next for me. I worry about the press. I feel bombarded all the time. I'm constantly on the road and tired, and even though we've run the miles and I've felt so far away, he never left me. Through all my mess, he had a message for me. I hid him from everybody. Even making like I didn't need him when he's the only one I've ever needed. He told me he was there for me when I lost my dad. When my dad died, I lost something that day. It died with him. And that hole was filled with hurt and disillusionment and pain, and a mother who stole from me, and a manager who exploited me, and a long list of bad decisions that I can't take back. I can just say I'm sorry. It's not who I wanted to be. It's not who I am.

My name is Mary Oxendine. I've not just hid my last name, but a name above all names. I'm so ashamed I never spoke what He's done for me to anyone. I never told how much he saved my life. How he changed me. I denied him but I can't anymore. I can't hide anymore. I can't live like this anymore.

And I want to thank Josey Wales. I hope you're watching this, Josey. The night we stood on stage together, I felt something break in me. A floodgate. Rushing water through my veins. The water that never runs dry. The spirit of the Lord fell on me, and I wanted to let the world know that night. You helped me, Josey. You were the one that tore away my veil. You opened my eyes. I want it to matter. My name. My life. And I want to sing for him, not for myself. Not for fame. Not for the applause. For him.

I love Jesus, and Jesus loves me. I won't deny it any longer. If you don't want to support me through this, I'll pray for you. If you support me through this, I'll pray for you, too. Someone taught me recently that everyone needs prayer, especially those who don't see the light. I'm glad he never gave up on me, and he's not giving up on you, either. So, if you've been running from Jesus, I ask you to stop. Stop what you're doing. Right now, just stop. Just call his name. He's listening. He's there. He'll love you through whatever mess you're facing. You aren't alone. That's what I want you to know. If you're still watching, I wrote a song tonight, with Presley Whitley, my songwriter. You'll hear it first right here. I hope you'll pray for me while I sing it. It's to honor my dad in heaven. It's my first song as a Christian artist, and I want to sing it for you. I hope I don't cry, but if I do, I pray you'll understand. Jesus takes the tears away, too."

Mary positioned the guitar on her lap and leaned in for one more prayer. She let all of her emotions that'd been mounting up overflow, and they had no place to go but land in her voice, as she sang her song for her daddy, and for all the world to hear. There was nothing about it that was easy, but it was everything she needed.

When the song was over, she put her guitar down and said one final message to her fans. "I hope you'll share this out with everybody you know. Maybe they don't know Jesus. Maybe you don't know Jesus. Thanks for letting me introduce you to him tonight. He's changed my life. I hope I'll be seeing you guys real soon. Merry Christmas and Happy New Year. Bye."

Mary gave a weak wave and saw the red-light fade. She fell back on the couch and let the tears fall.

No one moved.

Everyone was silent.

They let her take a few moments to cry. Finally, as if broken from a trance, Presley came to sit beside her and gathered her in his arms. She did let the tears come then, but they weren't the kind that are made from heartache but the release of joy. That kind of cry let Mary know everything she had said mattered, if to no one else but Jesus.

And that was enough for her.

Seeing Red

fter Mary received the recording on her phone, the first thing she did was call Mrs. Wales. She picked it up on the first ring. "Mary, is that you? Is that you?"

"Yes, are you okay? Is everything alright?"

"It's more than alright. We're so glad you called."

"Can I send you a video to show Josey really fast? I really want her to see it."

"Yes, and do you think you can come soon to visit. We have some news we want to share with you in person."

"Of course. We've already made plans to head to Tennessee as soon as the snow clears. I have a helicopter ride across the mountains tomorrow morning to look forward to."

Mary sent the video through text message to Mrs. Wales so she could forward it to Mr. Wales' phone. She wanted them to watch it with her and thank Josey for all she did for her.

It was odd hearing her voice through the echo of the phone. But when a young voice made its way through for the first time, it was all worth the embarrassment of hearing herself talk on recording.

"Momma, it's what I prayed for. It's what I prayed for. God heard us again."

Mr. Wales said, "He sure did. Even outlaws get a call through to the one upstairs."

"Can I speak to Josey?"

"Of course, you can. We love the video and the song. Your daddy would be very proud of you for that. And you know we're your biggest fans. We'll support you, Mary."

Josey squealed, "And we'll keep praying for you, Mary. He heard me the first and the second time. Do you have any special prayer requests?"

"Yeah, just to get us all safe off the mountain and find our way to you! I can't wait to see you and give you a big hug! I want you to meet somebody."

"You don't have to introduce me to Jesus, Mary. I've known him since I was five."

"Got it. But I meant my boyfriend."

"Oh, you have a boyfriend. Is he cute?"

"The cutest. His name is Presley Whitley. He's my songwriter."

"I can't wait to meet him! Did he write me a song yet? For the next album?"

"He'll be working on it soon. Merry Christmas, Josey. And thanks for giving me the courage I needed to do what was right."

"But I didn't do anything?"

"Yes, you did."

"Well, I think the prayer did it, not me."

"And the prayer came from you, right? So, you helped there, too."

"Okay, maybe I did. I can't wait to see you, Mary."

"I've got a surprise for you. We hope you like it. It's a Christmas present from me and my manager."

Lydia called out, "And her agent."

"And her songwriter."

"And her bodyguard."

"And her security team," the rest of the men said in unison.

"From all of us to you, Josey."

"Oh, I can't wait. Momma, they got me a present."

"I heard," she replied.

Mary could hear shuffling in the background. Mrs. Wales got back on the phone. "A nurse is here to take some more blood. We've got to go, Mary. We'll be seeing you soon and stay safe. We'll pray for that."

"Thanks again, Mrs. Wales. I'm sending out the video now. I wanted all of you to be the first to see it before it went live. I wanted to make sure you approved."

"We approve. One hundred percent. Merry Christmas, and God bless you, Mary."

"God bless you, too. Merry Christmas."

Mary hung up the phone, and as soon as she cleared it, she opened up her social media channels. "It's time to hit send."

She blasted the video link on all of her sites and uploaded it to her channels, her website, and every place she had a home online. "My prayer is that someone watches it tonight and finds their way a little bit closer to the arms of Jesus. So many people are alone."

"And sad."

"And hurting."

"And lonely."

"And scared."

Presley said, "Jesus is the way, the truth, and the life."

"He quotes the Bible. Randomly. Like just now. He'll be talking one minute and then out comes a saying that I figure can't be his. Like that one. See…"

Her voice trailed at a noise down the hall. It could've been anything. Or something.

Lydia said, "Give us another verse, Presley. I think we could use one right now. One about peace."

But Presley didn't speak because Jasper stood up. Another noise. To their left. He placed the tablet on the table and stepped into the adjoining room. He was back in about five seconds.

"Mary…"

That was all he could say before he went down. A knife protruded out of his back. Mary screamed when it all came at her. Full force. She understood but didn't. She saw him there, lying on the carpet, blood pooling around his body.

Mark had already connected with a 911 operator. Would they get here in time?

Presley grabbed Mary's hand and out they went into the hallway. He started to run with her.

"Wait, don't! What about Mark? Lydia?"

"They'd want you safe."

"But I need to be with them. Mark!"

She heard loud crashing.

Pop.

Pop.

Mark called out, "Go. Go!"

Presley didn't wait. He led her down the dark stairwell, his hand a firm grasp around her waist, never letting go.

They were down to the bottom floor. "We can't leave them," she begged. "Please."

"We can't stay here, either. If he's after you, then he'll have to come through me. But he'll have to find us first."

He stopped at the desk and leaned over, whispering so as not to alert everyone into a panic. The receptionist picked up the phone and started dialing for help again. Presley took two suits.

"Put this on. We're not staying in here. We're going out."

"In the snow? It's dark! We'll never see."

"Yes, in the snow. If it's dark, then he'll have a hard time seeing you. Whoever just did that to Jasper isn't playing, Mary. We can't stay in here. We'll get to the bottom of the road before he finds you."

Mary listened even though her heart was screaming at her to go back for Mark and Lydia. "Let me call them. Let me see if they're alright."

"Pray for them."

"Who's doing this?"

"Call 911. Now. Let them know we're headed down to the main road. Mark said there were cops already stationed there since the break in. Jasper made sure we were covered with a roadblock and assistance from the state police since the IP threat."

Mary told the 911 operator what she could. They were traveling fast, with Presley practically carrying her as they slid down the path, Mary's feet losing balance over rocks and uneven ground. Where was the road? The snow was covering it, and all she could do was follow behind him in hopes he could find the way.

"Hold on, Mary. It's not too far."

"But Mark."

"Mark will be okay. He can take care of himself. Just please, pray."

The operator reported, "We have contact with Mark O'Connell. He's okay. Paramedics are on their way."

"Oh, thank God."

Presley said, "Did they catch who it was?"

"How close are you to the road?"

"Presley, how close are we?"

"I don't know. I swear it wasn't this long when I drove up here."

Mary screamed out in a panic, "What if we went the wrong way?"

"We didn't, Mary. It was the driveway. It's okay, baby. We're safe."

As soon as the words left Presley's mouth a gunshot rang out behind them.

"Oh, Jesus. Please help us," Mary cried. "Someone is shooting."

"Mary, stay calm. You have officers coming to you. Are you still on the road?"

"I think so." It was so dark. "Presley, are you sure we're on the road?"

He had his flashlight out in front of him as he reassured her. "Yes, Mary. We're on the path. I can see the markers on the side."

"Mary, call out to Officer Sampson. Call out."

"Help! Help! Help us!"

The dispatcher came back on. "He hears you. He can't see you yet. He hears you. Keep following the path. He'll meet up with you."

Mary was too scared to cry. A gunshot rang out behind her again. This time she wasn't sure it was being fired in her direction. Everything was such a blur. All she knew was she was holding on to Presley, or was he holding on to her?

"I love you, Presley."

"Baby, I love you, too. It's going to be okay. I promise."

Her stomach started to grow warm and a strange sensation churned through her.

"I think I need to slow down."

She grabbed the stitch in her side that wouldn't let her go. "I'm…"

"No, Mary. We can't stop. I see the lights ahead. It's the officers. We're almost to them."

Mary couldn't speak. She could feel her heart thudding in her ears, the sound began to slow as the smoke began to fill her vision. Where was the smoke coming from? It was cloudy. Snow? Was it in her eyes?

What were the lights? They were bright. What was that?

A noise boomed around her, and the sky lit up with a red glow.

Thump…da…thump…da…

"We found them. We've got them."

Another voice said, "Call another ambulance. We might need an airlift."

Mary couldn't find her voice to ask for who? Was it Presley? Was he hurt?

She could only see the colors now. The lights flashed around her, the red, and the snow falling against her face, tickling her nose with wet fingertips. She felt a burning rising, all the way to her face. Heat and the whispers of snow against her.

That was all she knew.

Go Away

National Observer Entertainment Heat
Breaking News

Mary Bella, 21 – Shot, Critical Condition
Christmas Eve
Suspect still at large

Mary Bella searched her name, and nothing had changed with time. Her name was associated with scandal and tragedy. She scrolled through headline after headline. Every major news channel had her face plastered on it with the words…

Suspect still at large…

Ongoing investigation…

Nationwide manhunt…

Any information, call our hotline…

She knew who had all the information they'd ever need. Madeline Oxendine.

An accessory to murder.

Her murder.

Mary looked out the window of the bedroom. Mark gave her the best view, she was sure. Trees lined the new property creating a natural fence. A pine forest stretching for miles reminded her she was far away from red woods, and closer to home.

Mark and Lydia said their vows as soon as Mary was in the clear. They didn't have a ceremony but made it to the closest courthouse to file papers, wait a day, and then were right back to stand in front of a judge to make it legal.

They found their dream home days later, a fifty-acre ranch on the outskirts of Charlotte, a place where he could also make room for his parents in a home of their own. The builders were out in the strange, warm January weather of North Carolina. Just to think, a month ago, there was snow falling two hundred miles away.

Mary could hear the noise of construction.

Boom.

A knock.

She turned from the window and found herself staring now at the door.

Presley called, "Baby, are you up? I've been texting."

"I'm up."

"Can I come in?"

When she didn't answer, he took that as a yes, because he opened up the door and kicked it the rest of the way, balancing a tray in his hand.

"Room service, my love."

"You didn't have to, Presley. I could've come out."

"Are you ready for that?"

"No."

"I didn't think so. I do have an idea though, and I thought my chocolate pancakes could help ease you into it."

"Bribing me is a new tactic of yours? Usually, you give me a kiss. Let me think. Chocolate or kisses?"

"Wait, don't think too hard on that."

"Maybe I could settle for both."

"The girl who wants it all." He leaned over and gave her a sweet, slow kiss that took her breath away.

Every kiss was new. She fell for him over and over. Every day.

"All I want is you," she said tenderly, reaching up to grab his hand.

"I'm here, baby."

"I should make you run."

"Run? I'm not really a runner. I'm pretty lazy. Give me my journals and a piano, and I could sit happy all day." Guilt flooded his face. "I didn't mean to say it like that. You're getting stronger, Mary. It won't be long now. You heard what the doctors said."

"Spinal trauma can take time to heal. I know. Just give it time…"

"Maybe the Spirit was giving us a double meaning on that song."

"Leave me, Presley. If you stay with me, you'll get hurt."

"I'll get hurt if I leave."

"But you could be alive."

"I'm not afraid of death, Mary. Only afraid of losing you."

"I can't bear this. They've got to catch him."

"They will. Now, eat your pancakes before they get cold or you won't be able to judge my cooking properly."

"You're too good to me," she said, not really feeling like eating, but forcing it down.

"I'm not good enough. There's so much I wish I could do for you, Mary. I figure all that works is prayer."

"You're still praying?"

"Every hour."

"Keep praying."

"Someone else is praying for you, too. We promised we'd see her. I think it's time we take a trip to visit Josey Wales."

She threw down her fork. "No. I won't put her in danger. Wait until the fool is caught."

"We can't hide forever."

"Why not? Are you tired of me already?"

"Baby, you know what I mean. The doctor cleared you for travel. Let's go see, Josey. She still has a security team on her. Mark has seen to it."

Thank God her security team was still intact, including Jasper. The blade landed an inch from his spinal cord. Everyone said it was a miracle.

"I have the best team, and it still happened."

"It could've happened anywhere."

"What if I would've talked to my momma that night?"

"You can't play the what if game. That's energy you're wasting. You can't change that night."

"But what if I did?"

"You aren't listening, are you?"

"Was she going to warn us about Mitch like she's claiming or was she trying to stall me on the phone, so he'd know my location? I'll never know."

"Your mother is sick, Mary. Either way, she won't hurt you again."

Her mother was apprehended the same night of the attack and questioned. She admitted to knowing Mitch's plans to kill her, and she claimed she was afraid to tell because he threatened her own life if she did. That put her behind bars on attempted murder charges, not to mention the ten million she stole.

The FBI was now involved since it was such a high-profile case. Mitch was placed on a most wanted list, creating a national investment in the case.

Mark rushed in without knocking. "Mary! They found him."

"What?"

"They got him." Mark held up his phone. "Agent Marco's on the phone. They picked him up in Vegas. It's over, Mary. It's over. Thank God."

Relief flooded her, and she fell to her knees. "Thank you, Jesus."

Presley made his way beside her and brought her close to him. "Thank God."

"Let me go get Lydia and Mom. They're out back in the garden."

He ran through the house, yelling as if he'd had it bottled in for the past month and now it finally had a reason to escape to freedom.

Presley was still praying, and Mary thought she caught his words, but there was no way he said what she thought she overheard.

"You can't pray for them. Are you serious?"

"Yes, Mary. I am. I prayed for him to get caught first. I wanted him to never be able to get to you again. Now that I know he's in custody, I can pray for his heart to change. Jesus can save even the darkest soul."

"What if I don't want them to change? What if I want both of them to rot?"

"Then, I'll be praying for you."

"Get out."

"What?"

"Get out. I can't do this with you. You're some holier-than-thou saint wanna-be. Get out."

"Mary, I'm not going anywhere. You're hurt. You don't mean what you're saying."

"I mean everything I say. When I say it. Get out of my life right now, or I'm calling for a restraining order."

"Mary? A restraining order? Really?"

"Really."

He stood up. "I am praying for you."

"That's it. Get out. I swear. Mark! Jasper!"

Jasper was there within seconds. "I heard the news, Mary!"

"Get him out of here."

"Who?"

"Presley."

"Mary!"

"Mary, what's wrong? Presley, what's going on?"

"I prayed for Mitch and her mom."

"She's not my mom."

"Oh." Jasper shook his head and motioned for Presley to follow him. "You better leave. If you don't go on your own, I'll be forced to take you out myself."

"I'll go, but Mary, I love you. This doesn't change that."

"If you loved me, you'd understand."

"I didn't say I don't understand. You're speaking from hurt."

"I'm speaking the truth. They don't need prayer. They need jail."

"They'll get jail. Everyone needs grace and forgiveness."

Jasper grabbed Presley's arm and said, "Let's go."

"Wait a minute. You expect me to forgive them? They hurt Jasper, shot me, and would've killed me, you, everyone, for what? For money? For greed. We're lucky to be alive."

"And you have to forgive them anyway. If you don't, they'll haunt you forever. You'll never let it go, and it'll leave a mark on you Mary, that nothing can erase. Unforgiveness leaves a stain."

"Please leave."

"I'm going but I'm not going."

"You make no sense!" she screamed.

"I'll give you time, but you're still my girl, Mary. I'll wait for you to call."

"You'll wait forever."

"Then, I will."

Presley pulled his arm away from Jasper and made his way out on his own.

Mary sat down on the bed and fought back the tears. Mark and Lydia came in to celebrate the news, their voices carrying high with praise for Mitch's capture.

Jasper held up his arm to them when they came in the room, and they stopped short, faces changing in a split second.

Lydia said, "What's happened now? What did we miss? Is everything okay?"

"He prayed for them."

"Who? What?" Mark turned to Jasper. "What is she going on about?"

"He prayed for them," she repeated.

Jasper said, "Presley prayed for Mitch and Madeline."

Mark said, "Oh." Then, he went to sit down beside Mary and put his arm around her shoulders. "Would you have expected anything less of Presley?"

"Yes. I want him to hate them. To curse them."

"Mary, you can't talk like that. Be happy they'll get what's coming to them now. They'll pay for what they did."

"For eternity."

"That, too. One way or the other, ye can't run from the sins ye commit."

Lydia's voice was soft and pleading, "Don't be angry at Presley, Mary. Don't push him away. Trust me, you wouldn't want him any other way. A young man with a faith like that is hard to find. That's who he is."

"Then, maybe who he is, is not for me."

"Ye don't mean that. I know ye love that boy."

"Love can change."

"What if I tell ye, I think he's right. Are ye going to disown me, too?"

"Mark, you wouldn't. Mark, please."

"He's right, Mary. You can't live your life with a heart that can't forgive."

"Some things are unforgivable."

Mark said, "Nothing is unforgivable. We all were lost once, Mary."

She stared at them all.

Were they mad?

Was she dreaming?

Had Mitch not been caught? Had they all lost their mind?

Did they just not go through the same thing she did?

It wasn't Mark's mother. She was out in the backyard planning a vegetable garden for the spring.

He wouldn't know how it would feel to be that betrayed. That hurt. If he did, then he would understand.

She'd forgive them for not getting her. That's what she could do to extend forgiveness to others. *They don't know, Lord. They don't have a clue.*

What I Need

Lydia announced after dinner, "What you need is this trip to see Josey Wales. Let's get packing, Mary. We can leave tomorrow."

A week had passed since Mitch and her mother were both safely behind bars. The media attention was still hot, and she'd risk bringing Josey in it if she made a public appearance.

"Still a risk going out, don't you think?"

"Ye can't stay cooped up here, Mary." Mark stood from the table and started to clear some of the dishes. "Besides, we've got to meet with the bandmates and discuss plans for our new tour."

"Maybe not a tour."

"A tour, Mary. It's coming."

"And now you're the boss of me?"

"My contract pretty much says I am."

"Then, let's tear that up."

Mark sighed and put the plates down. "The anger, Mary. It's getting worse. You've got to let this go or it's going to tear you apart. You've got to find a way to move on. I'm sorry this happened. All of it. People are scum. Okay. They're bottom feeders. Rats. But not all people. Not us. We're moving on, Mary, and we're taking you with us whether you want to go or not."

Mary looked between them and guilt washed over her. "I'm so sorry. I don't mean to be this way."

"Then, don't be."

"It's not easy."

"It never is when you've got to deal with the thing that hurt you."

"How am I supposed to carry on?"

"Ye get up and ye face the day, Mary. For all the good it has in it. Ye make it count."

Mary's heart ached with the weight of it all, a constant pressure pummeled her like a fist pressing against her chest all the time.

"Let me call Josey. See if she's up for some company."

Lydia said, "Finally. Someone around here listens to me!"

"There we go again. I listen to ye, woman." He leaned over and gave her a peck on the cheek. "Besides, that little one doesn't need to hear my name being bashed about like I'm a stubborn ol' man."

Mary put her phone down. "Little one?"

"Aye, lass. Ye're going to be a godmother in about eight months."

"What!"

Lydia beamed, stood up from the table and threw her arms around Mark's neck. She peeked at Mary. "We're having a baby."

"Oh, my! I can't believe this! Well, I can believe this! Oh, guys! I'm so happy for you! I can't wait to tell Pres…"

Fist against chest again.

"Call him, Mary. Tell him."

"Mark, you know I can't do that."

Her phone vibrated. It was Josey's mom texting back that they'd love the visit and had room for all of them to stay at their home. No hotels needed.

"He's what you need, Mary."

"What I need is peace."

Lydia said, "Peace comes when you forgive."

"Not again. I can't."

"How can you say you can't? Have you tried? Have you prayed?"

Mary hadn't prayed. Since that night. Mark kept telling her she was in the shock of it all and soon enough it would wear off. He gave her the "I'm worried about you," speech at least once a day, and encouraged her to start writing or turn to her music.

Mary didn't need music. She needed quiet. The sounds hurt her ears. Sounds. Period. Words. They hurt. Words mattered too much.

Lydia reached around to the china cabinet and opened the drawer. "You got this today. It's a letter."

Mary saw the words she couldn't deal with.

Detention Center.

Inmate.

Madeline Oxendine.

"Tear it up. I don't want it."

Mark said, "I think it's my duty to check your mail for you. Let's see what it has to say."

Mary watched as he flicked his knife open and cut the envelope. He started to read it when Mary stood up to leave.

"Don't go, Mary."

"I can't deal with this right now. Let's go pack, Lydia. Didn't you want to go to Josey's? It's good news then bad. It's up and it's down. It's all words. Words. I can't."

"Listen, Mary."

Dear Mary,

I'm sorry. I don't know what else to say. I'm so sorry for a lot of things. I'm sorry I'm in here. I'm sorry it came to this. I saw the warning signs but couldn't face it. I didn't want it to end up like this. There's nothing I can do to change the past. I know you won't talk to me. I know you won't visit. It's better that way. I don't want you to see me like this. I don't want to see you. I don't think I could bear to look into your eyes and know what I've done. I'm a terrible mother that doesn't deserve to live, and I'm sorry. There. Take it, Mary. That's all I've got to give.

Madeline

Mary said, "She's sorry. Got it. Thanks for the bedtime story."

"Mary, ye will never forget."

"No, I won't."

"Ye aren't supposed to because it makes ye wiser. It makes ye stronger. Forgiveness doesn't mean forgetting. It's not making excuses for her actions. She's evil, Mary. He's evil. It means ye might as well be locked up with 'em both if ye live with this hard heart."

Lydia said, "You said you want peace, Mary. You deserve that, you really do. You're a wonderful woman, filled with love and light. You've got to find your way back to Jesus, Mary. He can be the one that breaks this chain that's locked you down."

"I know you guys mean well. I know you do. I'm sorry I'm such a mess right now. You've got to just give me some time."

"How much time, Mary?" Mark took her hand. "A day? A year? Three more years? A lifetime?"

"I don't know."

"It takes a second to pray."

"What if I can't?"

"I know someone who can."

"I can't call him."

Lydia held up her phone and Mary could hear the ringing. "But I can."

"No."

It was too late.

"Hey, sweetie. Yeah, we've got some wonderful news to tell you. Yeah, she's good. We're going to Josey's tomorrow and want you to come."

Mary screamed, "No!"

"Yes, she does. She's talking to Mark, not me."

Lydia crossed her fingers in the air and winked at Mary. Mary sighed. It was hopeless.

"Oh, you can't? Oh, that's too bad. We understand. Ok, talk to you soon. Oh, wait. Thanks for the email with the new song list. They're better than anything you've sent before. Ok, I'll tell her. Sure. Bye."

Mary felt it again, the swelling up of the pressure in her chest. The thudding in her ears. Her head started to pound with the rush of it all. Words.

He couldn't come. Or he wouldn't come?

What was she thinking? She didn't want to see him anyway.

Who was she kidding?

"I love him."

"I know ye do. That's why I told ye to call him."

"But he didn't want to see me?"

"He said he had some family business to take care of tomorrow and couldn't come. He just told me what he was contributing to Josey's promised surprise. He's getting her a piano delivered as soon as we arrive. All I have to do is text him."

"That was nice of him," replied Mark. "I told ye that guy was a keeper."

Mary carried the rest of the dishes to Mark and loaded the dishwasher. Lydia was busy texting and with each ding, she wondered if it was Presley or business?

"He sent songs?"

"Yep. New ones. Gospel tracks. Mary, they're better than anything I've heard on the radio to date."

"It's Presley. What do ye expect? Give him free reign talking about Jesus, and I bet they're phenomenal."

Mary had made the video telling her fans about her crossover into the contemporary Christian market and hadn't received much backlash. The media was always going to do its thing with her. She was used to that. But the outpouring of support that came afterwards, after the…

"I need to take a walk."

"It's getting late, Mary. It's dark."

"Are we safe here?"

"Yes, of course. But who walks in the dark?"

"I won't be far. I'll just go out back."

Lydia said, "Let her go. Jasper is close."

Jasper peeked his head around the corner, trying to put on a Lurch voice, "You called. And congratulations are in order, by the way." He reached out to shake Mark's hand. "It's the best feeling in the world. Being a dad."

"How's your family?"

"Good. My wife actually has family in South Carolina, so it made her happy to move. The kids have settled in at their new school."

"That's great to hear, Jasper."

"Let me go after her."

Mary smiled. "I'm not that fast. You act like I could outrun you."

"Who knows, Mary, what you could do, if you set your mind to it."

"True."

She knew where she wanted to go, so before going out she grabbed a blanket and her guitar from the den.

"Oh, you'll be awhile," said Lydia. "That'll give us time to make the final flight arrangements and take care of the things we said we'd get for Josey."

"Thanks for that. You know I want her to get that full outfit, and an engraved Bible case."

"I already have that shipped and ready."

She stood at the door, watching Lydia and Mark, finishing up the chores and already starting in on their light banter. They'd welcomed her into their new home, and not once treated her as if she were a burden, but like family.

"Can you guys forgive me?"

Mark said, "For what? What've ye done?"

"I'm hard to deal with."

"Ye're not half bad."

"But I'm not half good either."

"Yes, ye are. Ye're just dealing with some major things right now. We've got the patience to help ye get through it."

"Just give it time, again?"

"No better time like tonight, Mary. There's no magic time. Nothing can change the past. Nothing. Ye can fix right now. That's all ye've got."

"And that's a lot. A new baby. And you'd want me to be the godmother? But I'm not good enough."

"If I didn't love ye and knew that ye are, I wouldn't have asked ye to begin with."

"Was that you asking or just making the declaration that I was?"

"Same thing."

Lydia smiled. "He's a man. Go figure. Now, go rhyme and sing up some forgiveness, Mary. That's what you need to do. Put it all in a song."

"Maybe I can. I don't know."

"All you can do is try."

It reminded her of how she tried with Presley. She tried until it didn't go the way she wanted. It was so good between them, until she threw it all away.

Prayer wasn't supposed to tear people apart but bring people closer to God.

That's when she realized, Presley was the only one praying.

It was time she changed that.

That's one thing she could do.

It Needs Fixin'

The sun nestled down for a rest over Morrow Mountain and the stars had come out to listen to Mary sing a song she didn't know she ever could.

She climbed into the bed of her daddy's old truck. It needs fixin', she thought, and sighed. It sounded so country the way she spoke it in her head, the way Presley would've said it as he appreciated the old truck for what it was. A classic.

Her daddy's ride.

Mary spread out the blanket and propped herself up comfortably, counting stars.

She had the overwhelming urge to call him. Lord, what if he doesn't want to talk to me?

Call him.

But I messed up.

Call him.

But I…

Call him.

With every excuse she tried to list, the words call him were on repeat, like her favorite song. Except her song didn't talk back. It also didn't expect anything from her.

Music never did. It just was. Maybe that's why it made sense to her when nothing else did. It never wanted her to do anything but sing along.

We need fixin'

Like this old beat-up truck
It needs fixin'
And I wonder if you'd even take my apology
After all I've done
Could we patch things up
Paint it red
And live a little more
Take a chance and give it a go
See if it'll even go
We need fixin'

After the fourth attempt to type his number in, she finally hit send. "Hey. Can you fix a truck?"

"Well, hello Mary. What was that?"

"Can you fix a truck?"

"I'm not too shabby when it comes to my hands, if that's what you're referring to. Are you asking me am I a mechanic? Are you broke down? Where are you?"

"Do you think you could get my daddy's truck running? It's a 1955 Chevy, and I think I'd like to get it started up again."

"How long has it been?"

"Three years of sitting. It needs a little fixin'."

"Fixin' sounds like something I could try to do."

"We need fixin'."

"Are you writing country songs now that you're out there in the boonies?"

"Maybe," she said. "Wait, how did you know?"

"There's something about trucks and country accents and a starry night that might lend itself to a good country lyric or two or about a million songs."

"It was about us, if you want to know the truth."

"What were the lines?"

"We need fixin'."

"We do."

"If I told you I was sorry, would you take it?"

"Yes."

"That easy?"

"Yes, Mary. I know you're hurting. Remember when I told you I was patient."

"And remember when I told you I wasn't."

"Love is patient, love is kind. It does not envy, it does not boast, it is not proud. It does not dishonor others, it is not self-seeking, it is not easily angered, it keeps no record of wrongs. Love does not delight in evil but rejoices with the truth. It always protects, always trusts, always hopes, always perseveres. Love never fails."

"Please tell me you didn't memorize that?"

He laughed. "I want to, but no. I've got my Bible right here with me. Figured you'd need a verse or two."

"Or twelve."

"And why do you joke at me for wanting to memorize Scripture? Don't you learn whole songs without looking at the lyrics?"

"Your songs are easy to memorize."

"Are you saying they're predictable?"

"When words matter, they tend to stick."

"Exactly what I've been saying. I'm getting the Word so everything else sticks. Or the things that are meant for me, anyway."

"Do you still think I'm meant for you?"

"I know you are, Mary. But what you did hurt me. I'm not going to lie."

"I know. I'm sorry."

"I heard you the first time. You don't have to apologize again. I took it."

"You've got to teach me your ways."

"They're not my ways, but what the Lord would have me to do. I can't talk it without walking it, Mary. It doesn't work that way."

"So, you're reminding me that I talked all about Jesus on the video yet can't forgive, when He forgave me."

"I didn't have to say it to you, you said it."

"Forgiveness is hard."

"No one ever said it was easy. It's the right thing to do."

"For who?"

"Not for them, Mary. For you. It's not about them because even if you forgive them, they might not even receive it. They might not know how to. Forgiveness sets you free. They'll still pay, and continue to pay, until they seek the Lord themselves."

"I'm not telling them I forgive them."

"You don't have to call them up and say hey, I forgive you, to make it work. You never have to speak to them or see them again. You've got to have that conversation with just you and Jesus. No one else."

"What if I can't say the words?"

"Jesus knows your heart, Mary. It's that kind of relationship with Him that we want. He knows what we mean when we can't even find the words to say it."

"Will you come with me to meet Josey?"

"Another time. I promised my family I'd be there for them. My sister-in-law has a scheduled C-section this week for the twins. I need to be here for my brother. He'll probably pass out."

"Twins?"

"Yep, double blessings on the way to the Whitley family. More noise. Like we needed it around here to begin with."

"I guess I can tell you. Lydia and Mark are going to have a baby."

"Really? Awe."

"You just said awe."

"Well, it is awe."

"You're my awe."

"I'll get to you soon enough. I promise you. Write a song. Write one you don't have to show anyone. Let it be between you and Jesus. Lay it all down at the cross, Mary. He'll help you get through this."

"I love you, Presley. I promise I won't push you away again."

"I love you, too. But you might push me away again. Relationships aren't perfect. We aren't perfect people. We might get in a fight again. You might say something you don't mean. You might even get mad at me for only the Lord knows what. We can forgive, Mary. It's the only way we can be and make it work. When you love God before me, it's His truths that bind us together."

"I can't wait to see the new songs you've put together for the album."

"One's for Josey. I thought Lydia would've shown you already?"

"No. She probably didn't think I was ready. She was right. But now I am."

"I'll talk to you soon, sweetheart. As soon as the twins are born, I'll send pictures."

"And I'll take a video clip of Josey receiving the piano you're having delivered. I heard. I'm sure she'll love it."

"Call me tonight before you go to sleep and every night until I see you again."

"I do love you, Presley."

"I know you do. I love you with all my heart, baby. We don't need fixin'. But that's still a good title for a song. We should work on that."

Mary hung up, and a weight had been lifted from her that she'd been carrying around all week. The guilt of hurting someone she loved coupled with how ridiculous it was for her to wait so long to reach out to him was all on her. It was all her. Presley was just being him. She'd have to learn to take him as he was and be happy for it.

He forgave her so easily.

It had to be because he loved God before her.

She felt her breath coming easy. A feeling of completeness washed over her. *God, you've got to meet me here. Right here.*

Since losing her dad everything was so offbeat. Mary had to move but her timing was always off. She sang Presley's songs, but her heart was missing the meaning. She followed the steps, but the moves weren't her own. She wore the smile and the sequins and the façade.

Now, for the first time, there was a feeling like before. Before he was gone. She hugged her guitar against her and watched the stars taking shape.

She found the Big Dipper, but her daddy always called it the Plough. That was from his Robeson County farm days. They always started there. Then, her eyes traveled to Orion, who was more than just a hunter, but held the tools the farmers used. After that, they'd create names for the constellations and storylines that reflected what was happening in their lives.

What story could she come up with alone?

You are not alone.

She found Taurus and felt as if it were her free falling. She felt like she was skydiving. Flying. Knowing the Lord was tethered to her made the jump less frightening.

She didn't know how long it would last, but while it was there, she needed to capture it somehow. The only way she knew was to write a song or a letter with a melody. Whatever it would be, she'd let it live between her and Jesus. Never to write it down and knowing she didn't need for it to be in ink. Only from her heart to Him.

I've been so offbeat

I haven't been keeping proper time

My mind keeps replaying all the sounds of your goodbye

I've held it in for so long

There's nowhere for it to go but deep inside

Makes me wish I could find a way to fix it

But I don't have that kind of strength to let it go on my own.

Jesus, get me back on beat

Set my heart straight and get me back on my feet

I need a way to forgive them

For hurting me so bad

For everything they did and were about to do

I also need to ask for forgiveness because I've been holding a grudge against you

I've been hating that you have my daddy

And I know it's selfish

He wouldn't want me living the way I've been with an angry heart and my life just split in two.

Loving you and hating them won't cut it

I know I've got to work on it

I've got some fixin' up to do

Do you think you can do the fixin'

Because I can't get myself to work the way I need to

I need a heart tune up

A break in my pride

And give me all the peace

I might not understand but need

Thanks for forgiving me

Now help me to forgive them and you.

Please forgive me, Lord, for not forgiving you.

Signed, Sealed, Delivered

Mr. and Mrs. Wales welcomed them like they were the oldest of friends. Josey had decorated each room of the house with a handmade sign, sticky notes, cards, and drawings she'd be able to take back with her.

Mary was an only child, but there was something special about Josey that made her feel like she was a little sister. She let them all know.

Josey smiled, "I know why. It's because we're soul sisters."

Lydia was trying to hide her excitement but doing very poorly at it. "It's all arriving. Now. It's outside."

Mary asked as if she had no clue what they'd planned, "What is?"

Josey was no longer in her wheelchair but moving slowly through the house on her own. She opened the front door and let out a squeal!

"What's this? What's this?"

"It's for you. Your very own recording studio."

"Momma! Look!"

"I see, honey."

"Are you guys, serious? Mary, are you serious?"

"Well, I don't want to have to pay the shipping cost to take all this stuff back."

"No way! I really want it. I can't believe it. Daddy, can we set it up?"

"We've got people to do that."

Just then a sound from down the street caught their attention. It was two guys in a psychedelic painted van blaring 70s music, with the Sound Guru painted on the side of it in hot pink.

"On cue."

Mr. Wales said, "You thought of everything."

"Thanks for giving us one of the rooms in your house."

"Who needs a home office when you've got a singing beauty deserving the world. I never worked in there anyway."

Lydia was taking clips with her phone. She had plans of cutting a video just for the family, Presley, and the security team who pitched in to help.

Mary waited until Josey was preoccupied with the piano man giving her new baby grand a tune-up.

"Mrs. Wales, she's looking so much better than before, and to see her out of the wheelchair, dancing. It's an answered prayer."

"Her last treatment really made a difference. We've been praying one way or the other she'd have a quality of life that wouldn't be shrouded with sickness, but happiness. Look at her face. Pure joy."

Mary understood. "Music can do that."

"She's loved music since she was a baby. I swear that girl was singing before she was talking full sentences."

Mark said, "Sounds like someone else I know."

Mary smiled and gave him a hug. "Thanks for this. You know, you get some pretty grand ideas every now and then."

"And I agree with ye." He looked at Lydia and the love on his face was clear as the sky was crystal blue, not a cloud in sight.

"She's your best idea yet."

"Yes, indeed."

"We've got celebrating to do, Mrs. Wales."

"We do, too." She turned to Josey. "Go ahead and let's play the game."

"Go get the signs I made for you, Mary. It's a surprise."

Mary said, "I saw them."

"No, go get them. You'll see."

Mary picked up one of the signs. "What do you want me to do?"

"Go get them all."

Mary said, "Okay. Is this really a game?"

Mr. Wales said, "She made it up. Humor her."

Mary went through the rooms and collected the signs. They were made on different colored poster boards from hot pink, to purple, to white, the colors Mary always wore on stage.

Mary laughed as she ran through the rooms, Josey giggling like a schoolgirl with the biggest playground secret.

"How many did you make?"

"Well, I messed up a few. So, in total I made twenty-two, but really all I needed was eighteen."

"That had to take a long time."

"It took FOR-E-VER, but it was worth every cramp in my finger."

Mary loved the handwritten signs. All had her different sayings or Bible verses on them, or song lyrics. Stick figures of her and the band on stage. Each one was special in its own way.

"Are you ready for the game now?" Josey clapped. "Okay. Here's how you play. Unscramble all of the signs for a secret message."

Mary flipped through them, all out of order. "I'm not really sure I can."

Lydia had the video turned to her now.

"Were you in on this?"

Lydia shrugged. "Just do as the outlaw demands or else."

Mary dropped one of the signs and bent over to pick it up. She saw one word on the back. "Oh, I'm supposed to turn them over."

She started shuffling through them. "Come outside, Mary. You can put them all out in the front yard."

Mary followed them all, curious as to what in the world could this set-up be all about. Especially with Lydia still recording.

She laid each one out in the yard. "I hope they don't blow away."

Mr. Wales was there with a bucket of rocks. "Don't worry. I already thought that through."

Mary looked at the words. All jumbled up.

second – you – I – life – got – can't – something – imagine – another – without – my – myself -in – living – I've – you – to - ask

Mary walked through the posters, trying her best to unscramble them in her mind.

Mark yelled, "I've already figured it out. What's the matter with ye, Mary?"

"There's no way, Mark. You don't know it."

"In fact, I do. It's I can't…"

Lydia screamed, "Hush. Let her figure it out."

Mary ran to the posters and grabbed them, adding them to the front of the line.

Mrs. Wales said, "Imagine. Just imagine, Josey, one day you'll be singing *I'm Free* to the world."

"Imagine. Thanks, Mrs. Wales." She read aloud, "I can't imagine."

"I find it very interesting on how one comes up with games."

Lydia laughed. "That's it, Mr. Wales. Keep feeding the lines."

"I can't imagine myself," Mary called out each card in place.

It all started to fall into place. Mary placed the next card, and then the next card, and she looked up to Lydia who prompted her to keep figuring it out.

Mark tapped his watch. "We don't have all day, ye know. We do need to have some dinner soon. The spaghetti sauce is smelling nice, Mrs. Wales. I don't know what I'd do without the recipe."

"Thanks, Mark." She ran to the next poster board and put it in place.

"I can't imagine myself living another second without…"

Josey said, "I love this so much. I mean, really, I love it. Y-O-U are the best, Mary."

"Got it," Mary said as she collected the next one in line.

"I can't imagine myself living another second without you in my life."

"Almost there," said Mark. "I've got to…"

Lydia said, "Stop! Let her work for this."

"I am working. I'm breaking a sweat in the middle of a January day."

"I can't imagine myself living another second without you in my life. I've got to ask something you…" She shook her head. "I've got to ask you something."

Mary looked around and in all of the excitement of the game, she hadn't noticed a truck parked right along the curb.

It was a familiar truck. It looked so much like her daddy's.

She looked to Lydia and Mark, then to Josey.

"What was the game? What do you need to ask?"

"I already know it, Mary. It's what I've been praying for. He's got something to say."

Mary turned and saw Presley walking her way. He was carrying the keys to her daddy's truck in one hand and a red rose made out of crystal with the other.

"What are you doing here? I thought your brother was having a baby?"

"Well, technically, he's not actually having the baby. My sister-in-law is, and they've scheduled it for another day out. Change of plans."

Mary threw her arms around him, right in the middle of the yard, in front of everyone. "I love you, Presley."

"Does that mean she answered it, Momma?"

"Shh...I don't think he asked it yet."

"What do you want to ask me?"

Presley dropped down to his knee and lifted up the rose to her. She saw a ring in the center of the petals, two small diamonds framing a larger one in the center.

"Will you, Mary? Will you be my wife?"

Mary looked in his eyes, and she knew she'd found more than just a romantic, Bible-quoting, love-letter-writing, praying man who gave the best hugs and loved God before her, but a best friend, a love, a husband – for life.

Mary said, "Yes! It's not an I'll try this time. It's an I do."

"I'll take that."

"Does that mean they're married, Momma? She said I do."

Mary laughed through her tears as Presley slipped the ring on her finger. A perfect fit.

A song started blaring through the house and out into the yard. The music room was set to go and Signed, Sealed, Delivered: I'm Yours blared from the speaker system.

Mary took Presley's hand and whispered, "Kiss me."

"As the lady wishes."

He took her in his arms and gave her the sweetest of kisses they'd shared yet. She whispered, "You're my wish."

"Well, that was easy enough then. I grabbed a star and put it on your finger."

"I think that might've been my line."

"I think I paraphrased it. It counts now as mine."

"And what about the truck? How did you fix it?"

"All you have to do is ask, Mary. It took a tune up and about an hour later, good as new."

Mark said, "Now that was a proposal. Gotta figure out how to top that."

Lydia swatted him. "Too late, Mark. Don't go getting any ideas. We've got papers, remember?"

"I meant to do it all over again with you. I'm going to propose, then see you walk down the aisle in a big, poofy dress, and..."

She cut him off, "Then, you better hurry up figuring out your proposal or I'll be waddling down the aisle."

He put his hand on her stomach and leaned in for a kiss. "I love you, Lydia."

"And I love you, Mark."

Mrs. Wales said, "Now that you've all pronounced your love for each other, let's go back inside and cut the music down before we get a sound ordinance from neighborhood watch. I see someone at 209 peeking out the window on a phone. They might've already called it in."

"We'll give them a free concert if they come, won't we, Josey. Just you and I!"

"And I can sing my new song to you, Mary. That's my next surprise. It's called I'm Free."

"Oh, I love that title. And Presley wrote it?"

"Yeah, after he talked to me and Momma on the phone. Can you believe he just asked us some questions and all of a sudden an hour later, we had a song?"

"I'd believe it."

Josey took them to the studio and positioned herself behind the piano. She patted the seat. "I'm ready now, Presley."

"Oh, I guess I'm playing for the little lady."

"I've never had a piano before. I've got to take lessons. Daddy, can I take lessons?"

"Of course, honey. We'll arrange it next week."

Presley said, "We can video chat lessons, too."

Josey said, "Oh, perfect!"

Lydia was still recording. "I've got to catch this. Josey's given us permission to share it out on the sites. This little girl is ready to be a star."

"She's already a star. In my eyes and we'll name a constellation after her - Josey-o-peia. Let the Queen step aside. We've got a new one in town."

Josey laughed. "I love that, soul sisters and a constellation named after me all in one day."

"Pretty amazing day," Mary said, as she leaned in to give Presley a quick kiss on the cheek before he began to play.

"You ain't seen nothing yet," he drawled out with the country way Mary loved.

Josey began to sing, and her melody was so sweet and pure, her voice stronger than it was even on the stage, and then Mary was impressed with her tone.

I'm Free

There's no more cancer

Taking over me

I'm Free

Remission is the word that set me free

But it all came down to one simple thing

Prayer set me free

I'm cancer free

I'm free

Presley said, "Wait! I didn't write that."

Josey said, "I had a surprise of my own. At my last appointment, I got the news. I'm in remission. It's been thirty-three days. We planned this whole song, and then you sent I'm Free, and we reworked it to get you. Did I get you?"

Mary brushed back the tears, spilling over and dropping down like joyful rain. "You got me."

"See, Momma. I knew I'd get her."

"You sure did, honey. As sure as the Good Lord keeps His eyes on sparrows and you."

"Will you sing the song you wrote for your daddy?"

Mary said, "You've heard that one before."

"I love it. I know every word."

"How about a never-before-heard-of song? One that Presley wrote for me."

"Oh, an exclusive? Right now? In my own studio? Wait until Jessica and April find out. Those are my best friends."

"Are you talking about Before Me?"

"Has there been another song you wrote for me? For Mary Oxendine? Not Mary Bella?"

"I think we were destined from the start, thanks to your dad bringing us together and picking my song. I might have always been writing for Mary Oxendine. I know that's who I'll be writing to the rest of my life, except her name will be Mary Whitley."

"Let me find out you're writing songs for another star."

Josey raised her hand. "Except me! He can write songs for me, can't he?"

"Of course, he can! I was just picking! He can be your songwriter, too."

Mark said, "Can we hear the song? I'm hungry? And I think my wife might need to eat. We're on a schedule. The list says…"

"Tear up the list, Mark," said Mary. "I'm living in the moment."

"With a growling stomach."

"With that, too. Let's just sing this one song."

"I've heard this before. Ye'll be in this blessed studio all day and night."

"That sounds fun," said Josey.

"Okay, one more. Before Me. Then, I hope you don't mind if I steal Mary away and we go back home to support my family on the birth of our twins."

"Maybe leave that twin talk on the front lawn," Mark said.

"Hey," Lydia replied. "I do have twins in my family. It could happen. You never know."

"Nothing in life is a guarantee," Mary said. "You never know which way it'll go until you get there."

Presley began to play his song to Mary, and Mary did all she could to make everyone around her know that these weren't just words being sung.

It was a heart of a man speaking to the heart of a woman, who had finally found her true beat.

Thanks for Reading

I would love it if you could add a review online. Reviews really help an author and thank you in advance for supporting my work!

I would love to see your photos with the book! Please share social media reviews, and challenge others to pick up the series. Don't forget to tag me @jenlowrywrites so that I can join in on spreading the love around.

Don't forget to sign up for my monthly newsletter at www.jenlowrywrties.com to catch the latest author news, contests, and more!
Patreon Behind the Scenes Author Life, Pajama Hangouts, Author Gift Boxes, and More at https://www.patreon.com/JenLowry

Author Bio

Jen Lowry lives outside of Raleigh, North Carolina and is a proud native of Robeson County. She is the author of a YA contemporary fiction novel, Sweet Potato Jones and has her first thriller releasing August 2021, The Sunday Killer, with City Limits Publishing. Check out her twenty-plus published books and counting. You'll find her enjoying every second of life spent with her family (preferably in pajamas). If you ask her what she's reading it's probably more than one book. Learn more about Jen at www.jenlowrywrites.com and follow her online @jenlowrywrites.

Learn More About St. Jude Children's Research Hospital

If you would like to learn more about how you can help support the efforts of St. Jude Children's Research Hospital, please visit their site to see how you can contribute or pray.

https://www.stjude.org/

You can give in honor of someone you love, make a monthly contribution, fundraise, or go directly to donate today. There are so many ways to help. Let's give back!

Author's Note

If you, a friend, or a loved one needs help, please don't keep it inside.

There are family, guidance counselors, teachers, community and nationwide organizations that can offer help.

National Alliance on Mental Illness (NAMI):
https://www.nami.org/
1-800-950-6264
TEXT NAMI to 741741

National Suicide Prevention Hotline:
https://suicidepreventionlifeline.org/
1-800-273-8255
TEXT HOME to 741741

Atrium Health Call Center
1-704-444-2400

Mental Health Resources http://www.mhresources.org

American Psychology Association
http://www.psychiatry.org/mental-health/

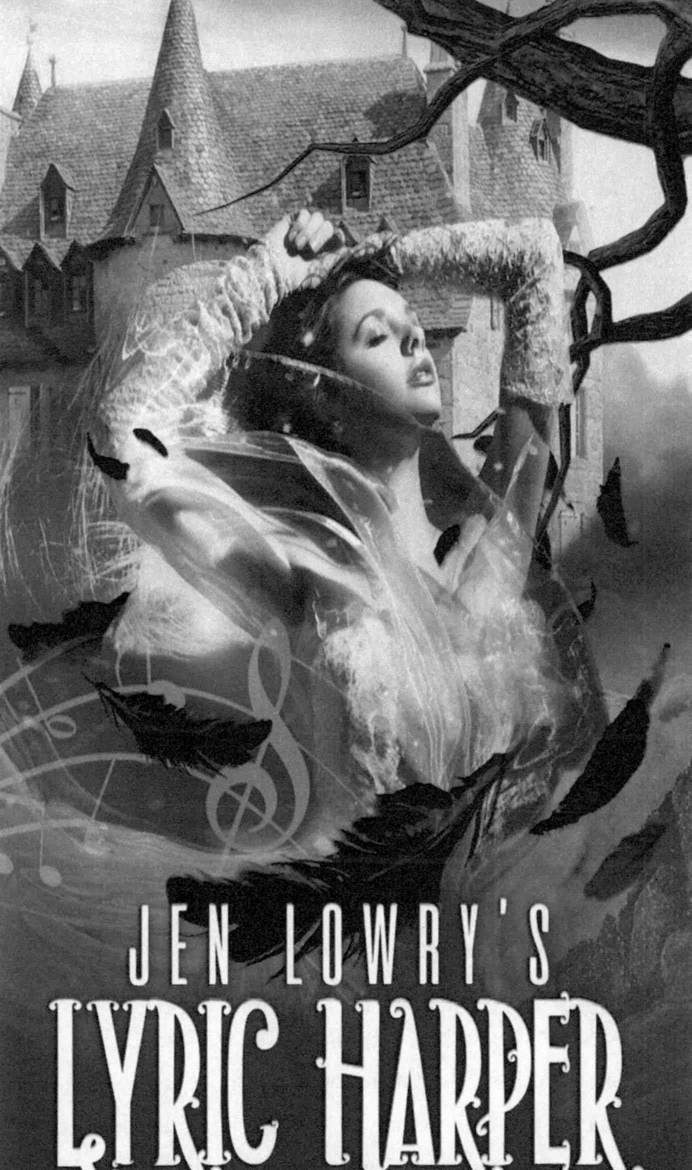
JEN LOWRY'S
LYRIC HARPER
AND THE HARMONIC BRIDGE

Sneak peak of the first three chapters of Jen Lowry's new book, Lyric Harper and the Harmonic Bridge, available in paperback, eBook, and audio.

Turn up the Radio

"Music lights up my life like nothing else can do…"
Song by Lyric

Lyric wondered if she felt music more than most. This could have been a complete misconception but in her mind that never stopped spinning tracks, she found that she often spoke in line and verse, and always thought that way even in the quietest introspections, beats lived. Those were where the rock ballads took up space. Everywhere else she rented out space to metal.

She watched for heads up to catch eyes, knowing that one way she could build her friend circle was to at least gain eye contact, but most of her classmates had heads down staring at the heels in front of them as to not catch a shoe. She stood by her locker and watched the robotic movements of hallway walk and wondered why they didn't want to glide, step, glide, step their way to the bus lot. Instead, they marched their way, scurrying like little ants, without recognizing their movements even had a way to be unique, just like their styles. They colored their hair pink and used a bottle of hairspray a day but they couldn't glide, step?

"Lyric! Hey, Lyric. Wait up."

Lyric stood still and found the command to be strange for one leaning by a locker holding it up as she observed the world and picked up the melody of the crunch of paper under feet, the swoosh of wind from a passerby, and the sound of the buzzing of the overhead fluorescent lights.

"Hey, Jonah. You see I'm composing. I'm not going anywhere."

"I figured as much. That's why I was telling you to wait for me. I want to try it, too."

Of all the students at Lake End High, Lyric found the most peace with Jonah.

"Call it when you hear it."

Lyric was training Jonah to zero in on the noises around him without closing his eyes to do it. Sometimes the filter helped to ease into the sounds, but for Lyric, she found she connected to the color of the thing and that might be what made the sound more vibrant in her mind.

"Locker slam to the right like a cymbal. Door swinging in the bathroom stall, creaking two down." He paused. "You know they should fix that sound. It lets everyone know when you are about to take care of your business. It's so annoying."

"Never. It's the eerie noise a house makes when it tries to wake up."

Jonah laughed. "Only you would say something like that, Lyric. Do you want to hang out after school? We're headed to the library for a study session. I want to tackle this project early so I can get my grade up in Social Studies."

"Who is we?"

"Josh, Lucas, and me."

"Nah. I'm the odd girl out. You guys go ahead. I'm waiting for something."

"Something or someone?"

Jonah's eyes narrowed. Lyric saw the flash of it and recognized it right away. Oh, no. Not the like gaze. She was a keen observer with an ability to break down a note, a composition, a spark of jealousy, or a look of like. This was the look of like. Jonah would mess this up for her. The only person she found she could step in with and be herself around was now turning out to be a complication. Junior year was tough enough on its own without having to deal with the pressure of the look of like.

Her cheeks burned and she tried to focus on the sound of clinking metal on metal further down the hallway. "I'm waiting for something at home, thank you very much. I'm just waiting for the hall to clear before I leave."

Lyric wished she could have said someone, but that would have been a lie. Jonah should have known better. She talked to no other guys except him.

"Are you waiting on the next line? I loved the last one. Piece of string tied to hearts. Don't release we are about to start..."

"I've reworked that line. Maybe the song will finish singing in me. If it does, I'll show you tomorrow."

"Can I guess who you might write it for?"

Josh interrupted his flirtatious remark. He had his baseball equipment bag swinging behind him, knocking into everyone as he walked by. Metal bat against the locker. The sound identified.

"Give me room. I've got practice people. Can't you see me?"

How could they miss him? He was over six feet tall and loved to brag about it.

"Hey, Josh. I thought we were studying today?"

"Did you really forget that it's smack in the middle of baseball season?"

"I knew picking you as a partner was a disaster in the making."

"Thanks for the vote of confidence, brother. I've got you."

"Does that mean I'm doing all the work?"

Lyric said, "Isn't it obvious."

She turned her head before smacking out another quick lash of her tongue. Josh always used people, for everything, but somehow Jonah found a reason to hang out with him.

"So, I've heard that Janie was getting kicked out. Is that true?"

He used people and gossiped. So likable, this one. The hallway started to trickle down to a manageable stream, and Lyric could move. She'd get the truth from Janie herself later. Not from some second-hand report that would have fillers without good intent.

Jonah called out, "Hey, I'll call you later."

Lyric waved in reply as she walked away. She could hear the subject change to her, and Josh asked what was up between the two of them. If only Josh could find his own girl, he'd get out of everyone else's business. But then, she'd pity the girl.

She saw her mom pull into the circle drive. Time flowed in tick-tock patterns separately for Seraphine Harper as it did for the rest of the world because her on time was always late, yet she claimed she was on the dime. Lyric watched as her Mother's fingers drummed the steering wheel and by the looks of it, the guitar solo was blaring.

Lyric slid into the hot seat and fumbled with the seatbelt as the next song started to transition. They only lived two blocks from her school, and technically she was about two blocks from everything in the town. Her mother refused to allow her to walk or ride the bus, heaven forbid. Lyric would've loved the time to scrape over concrete with the soles of her Converse, recording bird calls in her mind for a way a violin string might hit at the start of a chorus. Instead, the speakers blasted the new hit, "Turn up the Radio." and it was loud enough for everyone walking down the street to hear.

Her mom smacked her watermelon Bubblicious. She could smell it before seeing the half-empty pack in the drink holder.

Seraphine Harper slid out words smooth as a sweet, pink bubble. "You got it today."

Her heart raced. "Did you bring it?"

"No, it's on the table. The suspense is half of the excitement."

Lyric glanced out the window and watched the turn from the lot out onto the street lined with Elms. She wanted to roll down the window and scream to no one in particular and everyone all at the same time. The urge to do it was so overpowering that by the sheer force of adrenaline alone, she did just that.

"I got the letter today! The letter came today!"

Francine and Maddy turned their head and nose up at the same time. They color coordinated their outfits on a Monday through Friday basis, which Lyric found to be the absolute most horrendous thing to do. Gabe stopped pedaling his Husky long enough to look at her like she was insane, then went about his way. Lyric knew he was traveling to the pharmacy to help his dad with the counter shelf stocking.

Routines. So many monotonous tones in a world filled with possibility. And that letter would open that right up to her. Well, not the letter itself, mind you, but the answer enclosed in the letter waiting for her on the kitchen table that had immersed every daydream she had since finding out about Harmonic Arts Center.

Her mom turned up the radio right when the second chorus hit and Lyric sang along with the lines. It was true. She needed music as farmers prayed for rain. She prayed for the next line, the next note, the next beat, and strum of the guitar, and hoped there would never be a day when her music didn't work anymore.

And the letter could be her escape from her current world of the mundane of Lake End into a world of musical heaven that never ended.

A school that Lyric felt deep in her spirit was created just for her.

Lyric swirled her hair into her scrunchie, and the sweat beaded up on her neck. Her mind went two beats ahead as she clutched her Trapper Keeper to her chest, hoping it would keep her heart from escaping clear out of her cage. She leaned her head against the glass and watched as her breath caught on the pane as she sang along, making splash patterns as if she had dived right into a pool.

"Keep turning up the radio. We need the music. Give us some more."